Eddie the KIng
Stories of LA's Skid Row

By
Michael W.Corcoran

Author's Note on the Title

The title *Eddie the KIng*—with a capital "I"—is not a typo.

Or maybe it is.
That's kind of the point.

It reflects how things were down on Skid Row—crooked, off by one letter, and still somehow standing. The kind of place where nothing was quite right but everything still had its rhythm. People were broken, beautiful, half-lost and half-saved. You'd meet people with a remarkable history full of achievements and sometimes great bravery, and then you'd look at that person standing in front of you, just trying to get something to eat, a safe place to bed down for the night and wonder what happened, how did they get into this wreck?

The "I" is for the individuality that somehow survived.
Even in the wreckage.

Michael W. Corcoran

Foreword

I didn't set out to write a book.

For a long time, I was just living—working, drinking, scraping by, watching people come and go through the front door of a hotel that was more hospice than home. But when you live in a place like the Baltimore Hotel on LA's Skid Row for nearly two decades, the stories start to pile up. And if you're paying attention, you realize that some of those stories matter.

They're not all tragic. They're not all redemptive either. But they're real. Messy. Funny. Dark. Human.

I kept notes. Sometimes full pages, sometimes just a single sentence scribbled while working the bar, eating a microwaved pizza, or waiting for the cops to show up. Over time, those notes became stories. Some are about the people I knew—veterans, stuntmen, lost actors, street prophets, addicts, romantics, liars, and quiet geniuses who walked the halls in socks and secrets. Others are fragments of my own story, tangled up in theirs.

This isn't a eulogy. It's not an exposé or a redemption arc or a poverty tourism trip. It's just a record. A memory ledger of a place and time that felt like the end of something, but also like the middle of something else. I changed names, blended truth and myth, added humor where I could, and let the voices speak for themselves where they needed to.

I called this collection *Eddie the KIng*—with the typo intact—because like the man himself and like life on the Skid, it's a little off. Slightly broken. But still standing. Still telling stories.

If you've ever felt forgotten, invisible, or unsure of the path you took, you might find something familiar here. Or maybe just a good story.

Either way, welcome to the lobby, coffee is probably burnt, and the TV is busted. But the stories? They're all true. Or true enough.

— Michael W. Corcoran
Los Angeles

Table pf Contents

The Aristocrat

Mark woke up to his deep throated Chinese made, Underwriters Laboratories NOT approved alarm clock.

Beeb-Beeb-Beeb

It was 5:15 in the AM. He laid in bed looking at his Saharan desert ceiling. Waves and mounds of plaster, hovering overhead.

He lays there and thinks.

Thinks of his new baby girl, so close but so far, far away.

But mostly he just lays there.

Thinking is so expensive here on the Skid. It has currency, it's actually tradable on the S&R Exchange.

Thinking can get you in trouble, in debt, in jail, and in demise.

If done right, it'll free you, get you off the Skid.

Of course, doing it right is a razor's edge, sharp and unforgiving. If you think about THAT, you just stay, keep your head down and let the world forget you.

As you have forgotten them.

But now he has to get up and start his second week at his new job. No longer suffering the debasement of waiting to get picked at Crest Moving. Now he's an AM bartender at the infamous King Eddy Saloon.

It's a blessing and a curse that it is across the street, his shortest commute to work, except for that time in Angola, that was just 11 feet.

But this is ten times that and he's got to meet the Swamper, Jose' in a few minutes to open, mop and ready the bar for opening.

Bill the manager closed last night, so Mark expects a little seniority mess.

The shower is cold, the clothes are clean and the shoes are still damp from yesterday's keg problem.

Let's go to work.

The two men enter the bar together, quietly, like monks before the morning prayer.

Mark has worked bars all his life, although never having to get up this early. But whether it's 5AM, 10AM or better 7PM it's this moment when the bar is open in spirit, not in the physical. It's this time of fresh coffee percolating, the muted TV tuned to his channel, and maybe the jukebox playing free Temptation songs, 5 in a row.

Mark pours coffee for two, sits at the bar watching the tv and enjoying Mrs. Jose's breakfast burrito made just for *Nueva Marca*.

It's 5:59 and the crowd is starting to form outside.

Got to respect the clockwork of the alcoholic.

Mark looks to Jose' who nods, he then dims the lights and opens the door.

In a matter of minutes Mark is off. First, he fields the complaints of leaving the poor and indigent outside to suffer the hurricane winds and arctic cold of Southern California's unpredictable eco-system.

Once the masses exhaust themselves of the first round of complaints, the drink orders tumble out of their mouths with gusto and efficiency. A veteran lip reader would struggle to understand the unmovable lips yet coherent request of their heroic bartender.

"Gin and tonic, beer back"

"Jack and Coke, hurry"

"Draft, what's ever cheapest"

"Bottle of Bud, discounted, you opened late"

"Just a tonic water, twist of lemon and lime for me, baby"

"Two shots-Drambuie"

"What the fuck?"

"Drambuie, fuck, you are new. Bill never charges me"

"6 bucks Alfed. I remember you, Bill too, says you're a dick"

Laughter.

"Here's six and a case quarter for the effort"

"Dick"

That's the first ten minutes.

You're amazed at the old fuckers. Coming in this early, but when you look around you see this is what they live for. They get up early and are blessed to have a bar across the street or downstairs if they are the Elite and stay in the King Edward Hotel. Have doubts? No worries they'll tell you as fast as a new practitioner of Cross Fit will, if not faster.

By 6:30 you have a dozen or so hardcore drinkers. Mostly old white dudes. A few Latinos getting a little dose before going to work at the flower mart down the street. Sometimes you get a couple of blacks waiting for Crest to open.

The old timers talk of the days those cops getting off the night shift at Central precinct, two blocks away, would come in to knock back and drink a few with the many pimps that would come in before going home and counting up the nights take.

The women, exhausted, stayed in the pimpmobiles outside on 5th, sleeping.

Mark liked talking to the old ones, women included. Most of the men were veterans. They would talk about buddies, battlefields, and lovers. The last two with Korean or Vietnamese names. He recalled one old vet, Mr. Hansen, a survivor of the Battle of the Bulge, his entire tank crew were decimated in seconds while he stood outside taking a piss near the exhaust to keep warm.

He met Jimmy the Flea on that AM shift. The Flea was a man of tall tales, delivering them with style and timber. He survived Iwo Jima, ran with Chicago gangsters, and whipped his weight in wildcats.

There was Wilma, a late 70s former beauty queen and actress with pictures as proof. Pictures that would hold up today in any men's magazine.

She would sit at the bar from 6:15 till 7 dressed like she's going out for the night on the arms of Clark Gable. Unlike most of the older people who were in the Biz in their youths, Wilma never name dropped, hardly bringing up stories from the Studio System. Those were for her, she kept those fresh, never lending them out.

Your day would run on, with very little trouble finding its way into the bar. By 10 the OGs would leave and be replaced with the Game Show drinkers. These folks would wake up at a normal hour, watch the morning news and when the games began come in to start their day.

This was the beer crew, drafts and the occasional bottle. The tips were low and the opinions were given, asked or not.

This was 10 days after the Towers came down.

Mark would hear every theory as to why and how the towers were dropped. Only agreeing that they were indeed brought down on that beautiful September day. Got to think of the tips, not one's personal integrity.

Mark would pour drinks, monitor the bathrooms for addicts who would sneak in and count the ready-made packaged meals that he would heat up in the bar's microwave and sell for $2.

Bill really watched the ready-mades.

He watched over the female customers, which was effortless. Later when Mark worked nights, he would be amazed at some of the women that would cross the threshold. Some were trust fund babies seeing how the other half lived and getting their Bukowski cards punched for the kids back home.

Mark would smile at how many of these kids would ask if he read Hank always answering with

"Sure, who hasn't". It would be a few years later when he would hear the perfect comeback to that query: "Lived it, more than read it". Coming from a handle-bar mustache barkeep from the Westside of all places. Well said.

The day would speed up and just like that it was 1pm, shift change. He'd be relieved by Fightin' Leon who would bring his gal Mel-Mel by. Mark loved her company and humor.

Or Bill, bar manager extraordinaire, would be his relief. A no-nonsense boss in his 50s who could still throw down drunks or shots.

Bank was counted as well as the ready-mades and Mark would grab a shifty, joke with Mel-Mel and then head home to bed or mischief.

Mark liked his position behind that three feet of oak. It was something familiar in this new world that is Skid Row, it never changed from joint to joint. He was the bartender, the Aristocrat of the working class.

That's from Heywood Gould.

Pour the drinks, keep the peace, and laugh at the jokes.

Moving Day (and Sliding)

Happiness is always in context.

A billionaire gets a birthday card from Aunt Cathy with a Jackson in it—cute. A starving man feasts on a cockroach and asks for another. And a twelve-year-old boy, home alone, will jerk himself into a coma over the bra section of the JC Penney Christmas catalog.

My JC Penney catalog came in the form of an upgrade to Room 608.

Goodbye Room 215 and its scenic view of the airshaft. Goodbye to Chango, my reclusive neighbor who ran a six-block pirate radio station (KCHNGO) from his room. I'll miss the Tito Puente hour.

Farewell to my airshaft neighbors—forgotten old men assigned to the second floor so paramedics wouldn't have to climb stairs when the elevator failed. And goodbye to their caregivers, some of whom beat those men when they soiled themselves. I was tired of screaming at them anyway.

Hello, 10x12 deluxe unit with a view of the sunrise over Skid Row and a radiator I can actually turn off. Hello closet—with a mystery box bolted to the floor like some bootleg time capsule.

My happiness: abundant, if entirely contextual.

I never ask friends to help me move. If you ask someone to help you move, one day they'll ask you—and I tend to befriend people who live on the third floor of buildings with no elevators and a love of large marble accoutrements. Best to avoid that debt.

So, I moved myself. Late at night, when the elevator was mine and the lookie-loos couldn't take mental inventory of my belongings for a future B&E.

Skid Row is filled with people of startling aptitude.

The guy panhandling for change could sell real estate.
The dude sizing you up for a mugging could close a car deal.
And the woman giving dry over-the-pants handjobs while stealing wallets? Politician.

You always wonder why they don't use that hustle in the regular world and start empire building. But then again, the regular world never gave out as many second chances.

In just ten months at the Baltimore, I'd gone from carrying everything I owned in a bookbag to spending three hours making trips back and forth across my own personal Ho Chi Minh Trail. It was astounding what you could collect in less than a year—especially if you bartended or "slid."

Bartending at the King Eddy across the street, even for the short time that I did, had its perks. Alcoholics are not deeply sentimental people. I once traded two shots for a 1955 Fiat steering wheel. For a round of drafts, I got a hula girl lamp. Other deals included a cold mini-fridge full of government cheese, a wicker chair, and a pristine bowler hat that I still own.

But the real gains came from "Sliding."

Sliding is the fine art of scavenging a room the second a tenant dies or moves out. Usually, the desk clerk gets tipped off, waits for a shift change, then raids the room. Sometimes they have a partner, sometimes they go solo and take days to comb through every inch. The goal: cash, jewelry, drugs. All books and porn mags? Straight to the lobby library. That's the one written rule.

One night, Charlie the clerk handed me a key.
"Dusty just left," he said. "Slid out five minutes ago. Told me to wish

him luck and tossed me his key. Go take what you want, just grab his soldering kit and rocking chair for me."

Dusty had lived in Room 532 for thirteen years, a retired electronics repairman with a 1972 Simca parked on the curb that somehow never broke down or got a ticket.

I opened the door and was greeted by Doug the Viking, holding up a pair of matching pink bra and panties.

"Next stop: women's lingerie," he said.

"Jesus," I muttered. "He knew someone would Slide his room. Why leave this shit?"

Doug nodded sagely. "Dustine is feminine for Dusty, I do believe, my good Dynamite."

"Skinamax says yes," I replied.

We Slid the room together. Doug snagged a Selectric typewriter with extra ribbon, a cool scimitar, and the full collection of Victoria's Secrets, which he later sold to Melvin on 3rd, the building's resident transvestite.

I hauled out a Holiday Inn wall-mount TV the size of a stove. Doug said it was a Zenith Space Command SE2505-P. I also found a pair of brass knuckles, a velvet painting of a topless Spanish lady, and some decent booze.

Christmas came early.

But if there were a Sliding Hall of Fame, Maria and her cousin Anna would be its queens.

Until 2009, SROs like the Baltimore were considered "hotels" by the city and subject to hotel rules—two of which were:

1. Provide towels (mine was a single, ancient hand towel issued by Bob Rhollings. when I checked in).

2. Offer daily cleaning, which Maria and Anna did—on their own schedule.

Every night, they'd push their vintage carts down the halls. They'd endured decades of Skid Row tenants and all their filth with grace, hustle, and a little weed and pills on the side. If Doug was dry, they were your next stop.

They had eyes for the circling-the-drain types. If someone was on their way out—*estar entre la vida y la muerte*—they'd wait for a quiet moment, then enter, cart in tow. If the guy was already gone, especially on the toilet (Elvis-style), they'd start Sliding before the body went cold. I believed they were former KGB operatives, cash, guns, jewelry, pills—cleaned out in under ten minutes after flipping a room.

More than once, LAPD detectives would come knocking weeks later, tracking a handgun used in a crime—only to find the original owner long buried and their room long emptied.

They also cleaned up after suicides, ODs, and murders. I once found a copy of *The Good Earth* in the library with a clump of hair and yellowed paper stuck to the back cover. Maria saw me with it.

"Mr. Mark," she said, "that book is no good. That belonged to Henry. Room 439." She pantomimed a shotgun blast to the mouth.

Henry had committed suicide a week earlier. I was holding part of his scalp.

Charlie swooped in, took the remains from my hand, and slid them into an envelope like he was collecting baseball cards.

I took the book and left the dust jacket.

When a tenant died in the hospital or if the maids were off or at a KGB alumni dinner, the county coroner would ransack the room themselves— government-sanctioned Sliding.

And yes, all porn and books still went to the library.

My new room in 608 had a bigger bed (still sunken), an old blue dresser, and a mystery box in the closet. A few prybar nudges revealed a decommissioned toilet someone had just boxed up and sealed instead of fixing. A few months later, I found a copy of *1950s Plumbing* by Harold E. Babbitt in the library. A few weekends later, I had my own working water closet.

Moving out of the second floor—out of the airshaft, the screaming caregivers, and the endless death watch—was a turning point. I felt more like a human and less like a convict.

In 610 lived Paulie and Athena, one of the three married couples in the building. Paulie had been a paralegal until crack got him. Athena was a former B-movie actress, straight-to-video semi-royalty from the 1980s. She was kind of my type—more of a boozer than a junkie—but she had a kind of swagger I'm always a sucker for.

As they walked away, Athena turned, licked her top lip, and winked at me.

It made me happy—in a contextual sort of way.

Desks and Skateboards, Inc

The cheap digital clock-radio you bought from the electronics shop across the street wakes you with its gravel-voiced *beep-beep-beep.*

It's 4:50 a.m. You smack the alarm button, feel how hot the plastic has gotten, and without a second thought, reach around and unplug it. The bright red numbers fade like a dying cyborg. Peaceful.

You sit up in bed. This is where you've landed—fallen off the map, and no one seems to care. But that's not new. You've felt invisible before. Now it's just official.

Even people in freefall still have rent to pay. In two days, you'll owe Bob Rhollings—manager, prick, and enforcer of Skid Row's own Hotel Baltimore—$65 for the next week. No cash, no room. It's that simple.

You're broke. No phone, no car, no job. And you're a white guy—rock bottom status in this part of town.

Balancing on a makeshift stool, you take a morning piss in the sink and glance in the mirror. Late 30s, still solid. The shaved head subtracts a few years, and hey—you're about to have a damn good mustache day.

Nice.

You skip the shower, get dressed, and pour the last of your Black Crow bourbon into a wedding gift flask. Downstairs, you tap the bottom of the hotel coffee machine with your boot—an old trick. It spits out a bonus shot of espresso, saving you 35 cents. Oklahoma Bob, the Stuntman taught you that trick. You'd later repay him by burying his ashes out at the old Spahn Ranch.

Out the lobby door, turn left. Thirty feet later, you're at Crest Moving & Storage. Seven trucks already line the curb.

Looks like there's work today.

Inside, you check in with the foreman, Enrico—a squat, fireplug of a man with a temper and zero patience. The kind of guy who doesn't even get a nickname, which in a Latino crew is saying something. Normally, the moment you start shoveling gravel or taking down corporate empires with Mexicans, they give you a nickname. It's like being a fighter pilot, but with better food.

He gives you a curt nod. You're on the list.

The room fills with guys. Mostly Mexicans—surprising, given Mexico won a fútbol match yesterday. You figured half of them would be too drunk or too hungover to show. You'd been counting on no-shows to up your odds.

The unwritten rules of Crest: Mexicans get picked first, then Guatemalans, then Salvadorans. After that, the Black guys. Then, if there's anything left, the Whites. Asians never even walk in the door.

You're White. Nobody cares.

But today, you get picked. You punch your timecard and hop into the back of Truck #42. Inside are today's crewmates: crew leader Emilio, Jorge and Jose (cousins), Oscar, Louis, Pulga (tiny dude, with a freakish strength when women are watching), Felix, and Ricky—one of the few Black guys—and you, *Dentista*.

You earned that name on your first day on the job. Emilio had an abscessed tooth and asked you to pull it with pliers. You did. No hesitation. He made it to work the next day. Respect.

Ricky spots you and lights up. "Hey, Dennis, my man!"

You do a soul-shake-fist-bump combo.

"I saw all them trucks. I knew the white boys would get work today!"

Everyone laughs—even Mark the Dentista.

It's gonna be a good shift.

The work is brutal but honest—loading, lifting, hauling. You break for lunch on the loading dock of an old L.A. Department of Education building, being emptied ahead of demolition. The Northridge quake finally took it down, of course it took years.

Three Crest trucks idle in the sun. You and Ricky sneak off to take a couple shots from the bourbon flask.

"Thanks, man. Was wondering," he says.

You like Ricky. Mid-to-late 40s, skinny, smooth-faced, looks 25. He's unapologetically homeless, smokes crack, drinks hard, hustles when he has to. Family from South Central keeps trying to bring him home, but he prefers the streets.

After lunch, you're assigned to the seventh floor. Jackpot. Dozens of postwar tanker desks with matching rolling chairs. Gorgeous. Heavy.

"Hey Emilio," you ask, playing it cool. "Where's all this going?"

"Warehouse off Mission. Then the scrapyard."

You nod, then glance at Ricky.

"Dude," you whisper, "hipsters in Silverlake would pay five hundred a pop for these."

You both eye the desks. Heavy beasts, but worth it.

The chaos of too many trucks and bodies works in your favor. It creates blind spots, distracts supervisors. Time to act.

One desk is quietly rolled down the ramp and out of sight.

"Fuck that, let's get a another," Ricky says.

You grin. "Let's do it."

You upend another desk. A worker glances over. Ricky stares him down—hard.

The guy walks away.

Down the hill goes desk #2.

Perfect.

The workday wraps. You get dropped back at Crest, race to punch out. Elaine the cashier hands you $47.85 in cash for ten hours, minus tax. You sign the ledger and run ten blocks with Ricky.

The desks are still there.

Now what?

"We need a place to stash these. We'll take turns babysitting them", you say.

"Volunteers of America construction site," Ricky suggests. "I got a chill spot there."

"We need to be near a payphone,"

"Why?"

You explain your plan: place a PennySaver ad, they'll send someone to snap pics. They'll sell in a week. Boom.

You hoist one desk.

"Damn, we need wheels."

"I got you, homie," Ricky shouts, and vanishes.

An hour later, he returns, holding three stolen skateboards over his head.

You both howl like maniacs.

Two days later, two Silverlake hipsters with curly mustaches load the desks into their U-Haul. $800 cash.

You buy a beeper. A new white shirt from Kmart. Steal a tie. Buy a legit alarm clock. Pay your rent and stash some away for peace of mind.

Ricky disappears.

Weeks pass. You land a morning bartender gig at the King Eddy. Ricky stops in now and then. You pour him a draft. He never takes advantage.

Then one night, years later, you see him at the new Art Walk downtown— wearing a pirate hat, surrounded by laughing strangers. He's glowing.

You sneak up and smack his ass. He jumps, spins, screams your name.

"My main man Dennis! Where've you been?"

You want to correct him but instead you soul-shake, fist bump combo.

"I'm working nights at a strip club, Westside" you tell him.

He really lights up. "All that pussy, huh?"

"All I can eat, dude!"

He makes a grimaced face. "Damn, pussy eatin' white boys"

You gesture to his hat. "What the fuck is this?"

"Shit nigga' this is my new thang, my new hustle" He grins. "Got this hat a year ago. White folks eat it up. I'm rollin' in tips. Ain't that some shit?"

"You still streetside?"

"Hell yeah. You still at the Baltimore?"

"Yup. We should hang. Open that desk business for real."

His eyes go supernova.

"Fuck yeah. Desks and skateboards, baby!"

He walks off to his many fans, adjusting his pirate hat. Ricky the Downtown Pirate, a legend, in his element.

The Turk

Gun — check.
Spare mags — check.
Flask of Old Crow (full) — check.
Folding knife — check.
Notepad — check.
Dr. Grip pen — check.
Half a Twinkie's Snowball — check.
Book (*Dark Wood* by Christine Weston) — check.
Flashlight — check.
Spare T-shirt — check.
Bandana — check.
Loose toilet paper — check.
Handy wipes — check.

Stuff it all into a boring book bag.

This is a typical loadout for a bus journey across LA. Unlike New York or Chicago, mass transit in LA is an overnight commitment. The buses follow no known schedule—at least none plotted by humans. I like to imagine a concrete bunker above the city's tallest building, a war room of giant screens like in those Cold War movies, where Metro Imps plot new ways to break the human spirit through the cheerful automation of LA's streets.

Any trip over an hour has to be for survival, for love, for drugs—or for a favored bartender with a criminally loose pour.

Today's journey: Glendale. A long-forgotten suburb now riddled with cross-shaped megachurches, cell phone strip malls, and more Armenians than Armenia proper. Worse: no bars, at least none known to man or me.

Hence the gear.

I woke at ten, shit, showered, and shaved in the communal second-floor bathroom. Ate half a Snowball, washed it down with warm tap water from the sink/pisser combo. Looked at myself in the mirror over my ancient dresser. Not disgusted—yet.

I dressed and double-checked my loadout (see above), then waited in the lobby for the express bus.

Once on the street, you're a moving target. Rooftop snipers, bored cops, parolees with pop culture-induced racial beefs, or tweaked-out homeless with zero concept of "No." So keep moving. Movement is life.

Ben, a new kid from San Francisco, stands beside me. We're in that awkward pre-friendship phase, feeling each other out.

"What's up, dude," he says, eyes still on the sidewalk parade of hustlers and workers.

"It's cool. Ben, right?"

He nods.

"We're still waiting on a permission slip from your parents to let you be down here."

"Hey, fuck you and Dave Crazy. I'm eighteen. I can do whatever I want."

Good. He can take a ball-busting. Good sign.

"You should be in the Marine Corps at that age!" barks Bob Rhollings, the Baltimore's manager and full-time asshole, from behind the desk.

The whole lobby groans in unison. Byron, one of the few black residents and three sheets to the wind, slumps in a club chair and starts humming the Marine Corps hymn.

"Rangers lead the way!" someone yells.

"Where the Cub Scouts at?" another adds.

There's my cue, I bolt out the door just as my bus screeches to a stop. Wish I could've stayed.

Two hours and four transfers later, I arrive at the address scrawled by Margo, a woman I met at a bar off Lankershim last week. Just a name—Arturo—and an address off San Fernando Road.

She said it was a "sure thing." $9/hour. Mostly driving.

The place looks like shit from the outside: "Medical Waste Removal and Disposal." Great. Long-term, low-grade cancer, here I come.

Inside, though, it's all '80s Miami Vice chic—glass blocks, leather couches, and a curvy receptionist who catches me staring. Haven't touched a woman in two weeks, not since Shelly came knocking at 5 a.m. for ten bucks and a mercy blowjob. You are aware of rock bottom when you get head from a gal though a slightly opened door. Shame comes later—after the best sleep of your life.

"You here for something?" the receptionist asks, icy.

"Here to see Arturo about a job."

"Did you make an appointment?"

"Uh, no. Margo sent me—"

"You know Margo?" comes a voice from behind me.

I turn. "Yeah, she said come see Arturo. That you?"

He nods, holds out a hand. "I'm Arturo. Follow me."

I look back—Mariam, the receptionist, is glaring daggers, hopefully from Margo's name and not me. I wink. She growls.

Arturo walks me past a row of vans into a warehouse office space straight out of a mafia fever dream. Arcade cabinets, red shag rug, and a leather sectional. He's got the whole Armenian Scarface vibe going.

"You're Mark... the jiu jitsu guy?"

Oh, right—I was wearing my Gracie hoodie when I met Margo.

"Yeah, that's me. Been training a few years, off and on."

"I wrestled. In Armenia, we are famous grapplers."

I name-drop what I think are Armenian judo dudes—Miran, Miresmaeili.

He frowns. "Those are Iranian names."

Oops. I forgot Armenians and Iranians go way back... and not in a good way.

I fight back the urge to ask Mariam for some Turkish coffee.

"I like you," Arturo says. "You want to drive for me?"

"Absolutely." I pull out my license.

He hands it to Mariam, who makes a copy and glares at me again. I wink again. She growls softer this time.

"Before you fill out paperwork, how about a few rounds on the mat?"

"You wanna roll?"

"Just for fun, my friend."

He sets up gym mats next to the vans. Kicks off his Adidas and hands his gold frame sunglasses to Mariam. Probably just wrestled in school.

I size him up: three inches taller, maybe ten pounds heavier and NO cauliflower ears.

If he's weak, I lose gently. If he's strong, I still lose. It'll have to be to a tap; I'm not letting him take my back for a choke. No way am I waking up to Strap-On Mariam, the Pegger of White Dudes standing over me. I have to lose just right, this job and maybe—just maybe—a chance at Mariam is at stake.

He stretches. I stash my belt and wallet, take a pull from my flask, and remind myself to finish that Weston book, what a great writer.

"Serious?" Mariam asks from the sidelines.

"Just time us," Arturo says.

She flops down on the couch like she's seen this before.

We square off.

"Go," she says.

He shoots for a double-leg. I sprawl, spin, pull him into guard. He pins my shoulders, counts to 3 and calls it a win.

He fist-pumps like he just won Olympic gold. Mariam claps.

"Okay," I say. "How about we go till someone taps?"

He agrees. Confident now.

Second round.

He shoots again. I stuff it, wrap his shoulder, take him down. He squirms; I let him spin. He ends up in my guard again, trying that pin. I sweep, roll, trap his arm, and lock it. He taps.

Mariam is dead silent.

Arturo shrugs it off. "One more."

We go again. He comes in hard, yanks my head down once, twice, slaps me in the face.

It's on.

I trap his arm, roll sideways. He kicks me square in the balls.

Now I'm pissed.

I uppercut him, it half connects, his head snaps back. He tries an eye gouge. I drive him back, and as we hit the deck, I forearm smash under the chin, bounce his head off the mat, twice.

He's out cold.

Mariam screams as I get to my feet and walk over to the sectional and take a seat.

I end up vomiting all over the shag rug, couch, and glass wall.

"Arturo" she calls, slapping his face.

"He'll be fine, babe" I mutter.

I grab my ID copy from her desk and limp out barefoot, testicles swelling like grapefruits.

Outside and down the block a Mexican security guard helps me cool off behind a construction shack by drowning my bandana in ice cold water. I thank him, hop a bus, and try to disappear as an ambulance screams down San Fernando Road.

Coincidence, I'm sure.

Back in Hollywood, I stagger into The Spotlight, a gay bar where Cleopatra—a trans bartender I've known for years through a mutual friend—serves me drinks and deflects the twinks. I tell her about my day. She laughs until *she* almost pukes.

That night, I return to the Baltimore, drunk, broken, and sore.

Charlie is behind the desk, talking with Dave Crazy and now officially "Young Ben."

I tell them everything. More laughter. I need it.

Charlie pulls me aside.

"Room 608 just opened up. Bigger place, east-facing. Yours if you want it."

"But doesn't Bob Rhollings assign rooms?" asks Dave Crazy.

Charlie smirks. "Not to the Turk, here."

Jimmy the Flea (Bring Bourbon)

Jimmy "The Flea" Burns hit his drink maximum the moment he plopped his prosthetic leg on the bar.

"This is ol' Number Four—good for day drinking," he'd say with pride. No one liked Number Four. It smelled.

When we told him so, he'd wave us off. Once, Jabberwocky—a massive Polish man—grabbed the yellowed hunk of plastic and shoved The Flea's face into the big thigh opening. Jimmy didn't resist. He inhaled deeply, comically. The bar fell silent.

Then Jimmy pulled back, smiled, and belted out, "When Irish Eyes Are Smiling." The whole place, Jabber included, exploded in laughter.

Jimmy always set up his "clock": cigarettes at 12, leg at 3, drink at 6, lighter at 9. He'd walk in at 6:05 a.m., knock back five drinks, and get cut off at 10 on the dot. He'd cuss and moan for exactly 13 minutes, grab his cane (propped against his left knee), curse the Jap that took his leg, and hobble out.

And just like that, the bar went quiet.

His non-stop chatter was noise-canceling by nature—raucous, bizarre, often brilliant. His stories were landmines of truth buried in a battlefield of bullshit. If you asked how he lost his leg, he'd say, "Buy me a drink— hell of a story."

After a few sips for flair, he'd launch in: "Iwo Jima. Eighth day in, we'd just cleared a bunker. I stepped into the open—bam! Nip Type 92 opened up on me. Five rounds, shin to thigh. Me one way, my leg the other."

Sometimes it was a machine gun. Other times, a mortar. Once it was a rolling friendly grenade.

Some of the old vets at the bar didn't buy it—doubted he ever served, let alone stormed a beach.

Jimmy would just wave them off, not caring what they thought.

He said he grew up in Northside Chicago, ran errands for the mob, wore nice suits. Claimed Al Capone once handed him a yellow top for Christmas at church. "Wish I'd kept that toy," he'd say. "My aunt took a picture—I'll find it someday."

Again, the wave.

He claimed when he got back from the war, Chicago had changed—his old crew gone. Disability checks weren't cutting it, so he took a job at a pet store, then janitor at a social club that ran poker games in the back. After a big score, he planned to rob the place. But his buddy snitched.

They came for him. Dragged him down the stairs. His leg popped off. That saved him.

"Patriotism still meant something back in '49," he'd say. They took him to the bus station, not the Lake. "One of 'em stuffed a hundred bucks in my hand and told me to disappear. Semper Fi."

The wave.

He took a Greyhound west on Route 66— "Saw more of America in those three days than in my first twenty-five years."

Landed in L.A. Worked for the VA in Sawtelle, small town west of Los Angeles. Married Ruth, a script girl for MGM from Alabama. They had a son, James Jr., in '51. Lost a baby girl a year later. Said they took it in stride—at first.

Ruth got him a job working odd hours as a projectionist at MGM, but he started drinking more. Then came 'eminent domain'—their house bulldozed for the new 405 freeway. Ruth left with the kid. Moved in with an orthodontist in Sacramento.

Jimmy got an apartment next to a Culver City Tiki bar. Became its most loyal customer.

By '63, MGM let him go. He worked at the Van Nuys Drive-In. Lost that too. Rum.

He drifted to Vegas. Remarried—briefly. "Her name was Jane or Janice or Hickey or Gertrude... something goofy-footed like that," he'd say, never quite sure.

Did he say Hickey?

In '67, he got hired by a company that repaired drive-in projectors. They gave him a van and set him loose. He traveled the country fixing gear and frequenting sex workers. Said his only long-term relationship was with booze and prostitutes.

He even showed Mark and Young Ben an old black book. Entries like:

> *Sylvia – Baton Rouge – Big tits, smells good. $30 full. HAMster 4-6731*
> *Diane & Peggy – Cincinnati – Big asses. Negroes. $40 for both. 513-555-9087*
> *J.J. – Oakland – Ass only, great BJs, bring bourbon. $20 (could be a fella), no phone, Clay & 8th.*

They always loved that last one: *"Bring bourbon (could be a fella)."*

By the '80s, drive-ins were closing. He tried his luck at multiplexes but couldn't adapt. Back to L.A. Rented a room at the Baltimore—just for a month. Stayed 18 years.

He did temp typing gigs, banged his plastic leg on the bar, and got cut off by the bald bartender—Mark.

Later he always apologized. He liked Mark, called him a great listener.

One time, Mark and Jimmy took the bus to Santa Monica to catch a special screening of *The Best Years of Our Lives*. On the way, Jimmy pointed out old haunts, his first house, his favorite bars.

The film moved them both.

On the ride back, Jimmy grew quiet. Pointed to a cemetery far off.

"My little girl is buried there. I'll be 80 next year. Wonder if she'll recognize me."

Mark, caught off guard, nodded—choking back tears.

Six weeks later, Jimmy "The Flea" Burns died at Good Samaritan. Mark, Young Ben, and Johnny rushed to the hospital. He was already gone.

Two weeks after, Mark returned from work to find a familiar-looking man at the front desk.

"This is James," said Terry. "Jimmy's son."

Spitting image. They shook hands. Jimmy's ghost in street clothes.

James needed to collect his father's things. Terry couldn't leave the desk.

"Mark, can you take him up?"

Inside the room, it was tidy. First time either had seen it.

There was a blue Marine Corps Iwo Jima veterans cap. Photos: a young Jimmy in boot camp. Later, grinning with other jarheads in what looked like a tropical hellhole. Another of him receiving a Purple Heart while in a hospital bed.

A black-and-white of a young well-dressed Jimmy outside Wrigley Field. One of him and Ruth on Venice Pier, toddler James in tow.

"That's Mom and Dad—and me. I think I was three," James said, pocketing the picture.

Mark gestured to the wall. "No Al Capone photo?"

James laughed. "My mom's got that one. Might be him. He's dressed like Santa Claus."

Mark glanced at his watch. "Hey, if you find a black book of phone numbers, can you leave it downstairs with Terry? It's mine. I let him borrow it."

James nodded, distracted.

Mark thought about asking for the pictures—to shove them in the face of every doubter at the bar. But he knew Jimmy could've done that himself. He didn't.

Because he never gave a damn what anyone thought.

And Mark never got that black book.

The Book of Luke

It was the summer of 1985 when Charles Luke wandered into the lobby of the Baltimore Hotel. He was 35, jobless, and on the run—not from the law, but from responsibility. Most would've called him lazy. Charlie just didn't care. Wake up, get through the day, sleep, repeat. No ambition, no goals, but also no real malice. He wasn't adding anything to the world, but he wasn't subtracting either.

That day, holding a folded classifieds section under his arm, Charlie found something in the stale air of the Baltimore that made time seem to slow down. As if life had taken a breather and invited him to exit through the gift shop. Within twenty minutes, he landed the night desk job. Room included. Half rent. Twenty bucks a week.

Eighteen years later, Mark would ask him if he ever thought he'd still be there, pushing mail and watching the front door.

"Yup," he said. "First time I saw all the bums in the lobby; I knew expectations were low."

Skid Row in '85 was the tail end of the original wave—old white men clinging to a world that had stopped asking anything of them. The bars lined up like gravestones: King Eddy, Torchy's, The Hold Out, Crabby Joe's, The Lariat. A man could crawl from one end of 5th Street to the other and never be sober. Alcohol was the anchor that held the place together. It was consumed, pissed, and puked within ten feet of every purchase.

Charlie took every shift he could those first ten years. When he wasn't behind the counter, he was walking to the Central Library or heading out to Hollywood metal clubs.

"Never really drank or did drugs," he told Mark once. "Probably the only sober guy in the room. But I loved the scene. The music. The women. God, I loved those women."

"Did you ever hook up with any of them?" Mark asked.

"Nope."

Mark used to picture him in those clubs—motionless in a sea of flailing black leather and hair, just this stocky, immovable shape in the chaos. Even in his fifties, Charlie looked like a brick wall. Six feet tall and built like a refrigerator.

As the hair metal faded, so did his trips to the Strip. His world shrank to the block. Grocery runs for bologna, cookies, and roll-your-own tobacco. He stopped shaving. Teeth yellowed. Veneers followed. He'd start his shift at 10 p.m., off at 6 a.m. By the early 2000s, he was basically a shut-in.

He had a daughter—sort of. Back in the late '80s, he'd traded a few months of nightly handjobs for turning a blind eye to a peep-show prostitute's side hustle. One night she let him use her "vagina," as he clinically put it. Nine months later, a girl was born.

He never met her, but like clockwork, he sent a hundred bucks a month. Guilt? Maybe. Habit? More likely.

In the early 2000s, she reached out. Letters. Poems. She was sixteen and lonely, the daughter of a sex worker in South Seattle. He wrote back. Told her about Skid Row, the drunks, the ghosts, the slow erosion of downtown.

She found it romantic. His words had grit, smelled like something real.

Then the letters changed.

The poems stopped. Photos started arriving. Bikinis. Then nude. Then her with other girls, older women—posing. Poses he asked for.

Charlie started slipping. He began watching porn on the lobby's front desk TV. Didn't care who was around. Just sat there, shirtless some nights, belly hanging over his belt, surrounded by stacks of old porn tapes and VHS boxes with no covers.

His kingdom of static and cum-stained plastic.

He used to joke that the Baltimore was his monastery—his quiet life of no demands, no connection. But by the end, even he couldn't pretend it wasn't a tomb.

Still, he stayed. Because nothing was expected. And for Charles Luke, that was as close to peace as he'd ever get.

The only speed bump in his low-impact life was dealing with Bob Rhollings during Monday and Tuesday shift changes. He'd known Bob for seven years, since he was first hired as manager. Bob didn't like Charlie's no-fucks-given attitude, or the way he ran his night shifts— leaving the lobby door unlocked, lights on, basically inviting trouble in.

Bob hated the fact that the owner, Willie, didn't care what he thought.

Charlie stayed.

It got worse between them when Bob gave one of the new residents— Mark, the bartender from the King Eddy—a better room Charlie had vouched for. Mark was in the building's air shaft room, 215. Then out of nowhere, he's in 608. Bigger, cleaner, just seven bucks more a month.

Mark didn't belong there, Bob thought. He wasn't desperate. He wasn't a raging alcoholic.

Bob couldn't push him around.

Worse, Bob heard that Charlie, Mark, Dave Crazy, and a new tenant named Ben were holding nightly shit-talking meetings in the lobby.

Bob would seethe thinking about them conspiring in the early hours. Plotting against him. Waiting for Charlie to screw up.

He was right to wait. He just didn't think it would take three years.

When Mark thinks back to those nights—talking with Young Ben, Dave Crazy, and Charles Luke in the lobby—he wishes he'd given their little clique a name. Something cringey but fitting. The Skid Row Philosophers. The AM Shit Talkers. Anything to set them apart from the zombie hordes that drifted past the window, to and from committing the various crimes that make LA its own paradox.

They could start the night debating the impact of 9/11 on Vietnamese taxi driver's insurance premiums (they did) and end it with the pros and cons of Seka retiring from porn and moving to Chicago (Mark was against it—she would've made a great porn director).

The quad continued gathering for about three years. Charlie came out of his funk. He shelved the porn. Toned it down with his daughter. Even let Mark burn the polaroids in a ceremony he said he learned from the Zulu.

And then the beginning of the end showed up in a Maybach.

Young Ben's father arrived flanked by two plainclothes cops and a Mercedes so expensive it had a new name. They pulled up outside just as Pope John Paul II took his final breath.

Terry, the morning desk clerk, watched from behind the front desk. The car door opened. He froze. No escape.

"They must be here for me," Terry thought.

He'd skipped a PO meeting. Owed Danny the Dyke two hundred from a February UFC fight, but she wouldn't send a Maybach enforcer. Maybe someone on Amber's List called in a prank.

Too late. They were inside.

"I need access to Benjamin Stanning's room. This is the boy's father," said the officer, flashing his badge.

Terry glanced at the man in a Brioni suit and handed over the key.

"Room 246, in the back."

"Yes, we know."

Minutes later, Young Ben was quietly escorted into the Maybach and whisked back to his family's San Francisco estate.

One down. Three to go.

Dave Crazy became a grandfather not long after that. Changed shifts at the psych hospital so he could be the kind of grandparent everyone wants: needed.

Mark got a job at a strip club, catching glimpses of Charlie once or twice a week.

Charlie drifted back into himself. Quiet. Withdrawn. Rolling his own cigs. Watching the streets change through the lobby glass.

He even locked the door.

Eventually, he confiscated a motorized wheelchair from a recently deceased tenant. It was more like a tiny car. He took it on the Metro handicapped buses, back to his old haunts on the Strip. He rode it everywhere.

He saw no need to walk, so his legs saw no need to exist. By 2006, he was diagnosed with Peripheral Artery Disease from his diabetes and sedentary lifestyle.

"We must remove your legs. Today."

Mark got the call on a dusty landline he still had. It seldom rang.

"They want to cut my legs off. Today. Before 4."

Mark picked him up an hour later. Charlie was sitting in the grass outside General Hospital, glaring at his legs.

It was a quiet ride back. He mumbled curses to the wheelchair gods.

Mark helped him out of the truck at the hotel. Bob Rhollings stood outside smoking. It was the first time Mark had ever touched Charlie, a man he'd seen nearly every day for four years.

He thought of E. Peabody.

"What do you want me to do with the wheelchair?" Mark asked.

"Give it to some dumb fucking asshole," Charlie snapped.

They looked over at Rhollings and laughed.

It was a good laugh.

Two months later, Mark heard that Charlie got transferred to the night desk across the street at the King Edward Hotel. Might as well have sent him to Mars.

Apparently, Bob finally got his revenge. Fired Charlie for some trumped-up theft charge. Charlie sued, won, and got free housing in any of the owner's properties. Baltimore or King Edward. He chose the desk job.

Bob was fired.

Be careful what you ask for.

After a tearful call to his retired college professor parents, they sent Charlie money to see a specialist at Cedars-Sinai.

A few months later, Charlie had his legs back—and made sure everyone knew it.

He became Charlie 3000. His nights at King Edward were filled with him dancing around the lobby to Frank Sinatra and ALL the disco. Tenants complained. The owner—still salty about the Turkish activist lawyer Charlie hired—just said:

"Let the fucker dance."

Dave Crazy checked in from time to time, confirming the transformation.

One Sunday, Mark saw Charlie on the 720 Metro bench, smiling into space, clutching a big blue Bible, dressed to the nines.

"On the way to church, are we?" Mark yelled.

Charlie nodded, never losing the smile, then jumped up and pointed the book at Mark.

"Have YOU taken Jesus as your Lord and Sav—"

Mark peeled out like the God of the Gut.

Over a year passed.

Then one cold January morning in 2007, Mark was walking to his parking deck.

"Mark. Mark Ringo?" a timid voice called from the mass of homeless loitering nearby.

He froze. Not many knew his nom de guerre.

It was Charlie. Sitting against the wall. Down to 160 pounds, long white beard, barefoot. His feet were so black only the yellow toenails gave them away.

"Charlie?"

He smiled—a big, black, veneer-less smile. His eyes were gone. The sidewalk had taken him.

"You're going to Hell, Mark Ringo."

"Looks like you're already there, buddy."

Mark turned and walked off, knowing the longer he stayed, the better target he made.

He never saw Charles Luke again.

Fightin' Leon

Could a man be this tough?
Not just any man—but a 61-year-old man?

He wore his white hair and beard like an afterthought—almost like a lion's mane. His bulbous forehead had long since won the receding war, pushing his hairline back to near the top of his head. And since it was the same red as his alcoholic's nose, it looked like the surface of Mars—canals included.

Yeah, a man could.
Probably why they called him "Fightin' Leon."

He stood five-foot-eight on a good day (sober). Less, when he was saucing it up—as his girlfriend Mel-Mel liked to say.

They lived on the second floor of the Baltimore, facing the King Eddie Saloon—where Leon and I worked, and where Mel-Mel drank until her soaps came on in the afternoon.

Living on the second floor was a nightmare, unless you were deaf or mentally derelict. The constant yelling and bus noise would *make* you one, if you stuck around long enough.

Young Ben lived on the second too—but in the back, facing the alley. He bought his nightly solitude by firing bottles of piss at the junkies and drunks arguing below. "Mostly works," he told me. But when it didn't, he could count on chunks of busted alley pavement hurled back with terrifying accuracy through his window—sending him into fits of laughter.

But *Fightin' Leon* loved the second.
I found out why one day.

I was heading down the stairs and saw the maintenance man, Doug, working in room 204—door wide open.

Now, 204 is a dead room. Never rented out because the toilet floods. It's just kept vacant.

In the Baltimore Hotel, there are *exactly* four dead rooms:

- 204

- 304 (same plumbing curse)

- 313 (haunted?)

- and 365A in the Annex, used for film shoots or LAPD stakeouts on Main Street. (Don't tell anyone.)

Sometimes the narcs left behind their binoculars—considered a gift from the gods. Good gear. Tax dollars going the extra mile.
Back in the day, old timers said they'd find beer cans and porn mags in there after the cops cleared out. *That's* an extra mile.

Anyway, 204 was also the unofficial storage closet for cleaning carts—this *was* still technically a hotel.

Doug was stoned and poking through the clutter. I stepped in to chat.

"What's that?" I asked, pointing to a small TV in the corner.

"That is a television set from the 1970s. And I don't have any weed, so don't ask."

"From the '70s?"

"Yes."

"How do you know? That's so specific, dude."

Doug the Viking inhaled deeply and stuck his thumbs into his overall straps like a Southern statesman.

"It's a Motorola Series 9 solid state television. Discontinued in 1974."

"No kidding. How much is it worth?"

"The pawn shop downstairs will give you five bucks. One of the hookers on Spring Street will give you one—blow job."

I grinned. I love to press.

"So, no weed?" I patted his overall pockets.

Doug stood his ground like a champ.

"No, Dynamite. I have no weed. And if you touch me again, I'll see you hanged."

I gave up asking why he called me *Dynamite* a long time ago.

"Alright, tough guy. Does it work?"

He stooped, picked up the relic, and plugged it in. It came to life immediately—sharp black and white picture. The reception was crystal. A noon newscast, only in grayscale.

We turned the dial through the VHF channels, then landed on UHF— and suddenly, Fightin' Leon's love for the second floor came into *black-and-white* focus.

We were looking directly into Leon and Mel-Mel's apartment in 205. A hidden camera view. High up, probably atop a kitchen cabinet.

I started connecting dots.

I opened the bar three days a week at 6 a.m.
At noon, Leon and Mel-Mel would wander in—Leon carrying a small black TV. (A Lenco T-9030 mini, according to Doug.)

Leon would place the set behind the bar, under a cloth curtain. Folks figured he was watching sports. Throughout his shift, after Mel-Mel left, he'd peek under the curtain.

Sometimes nothing.

Sometimes, after a peek, he'd explode—jump the bar, sprint across the street, up the stairs, and into his room, yelling at Mel-Mel.
Then he'd come back, muttering to himself, and resume mid-pour or mid-conversation.

Apparently, with his black-and-white eye, he'd catch her on the phone, or talking to someone at the door—and that was enough to send him sprinting like Jesse Owens in a rage.

When we moved the TV even an inch, the feed was gone.

"This is the perfect spot right here," Doug said. "The gods are generous today, Dynamite."

I nodded, still stunned.

"Yeah, Doug. This explains a lot about ol' Leon. You think Mel-Mel knows?"

"Nope."

The next few weeks, anytime I saw the flicker of lights under 204, I'd knock lightly. Doug would let me in. We'd sit on milk crates, eating burritos, watching *Mel-Mel and Leon* eat burritos and watch TV.

It became like heroin.

One night we watched Mel-Mel rail Fightin' Leon in the ass with a huge black strap-on. His grunts echoed through the hundred-year-old fireproof walls.

Doug took a long pull from his Diet Dr Pepper.

"Damn, Dynamite," he said. "Fightin' Leon sure is one tough man."

This Flat Earth

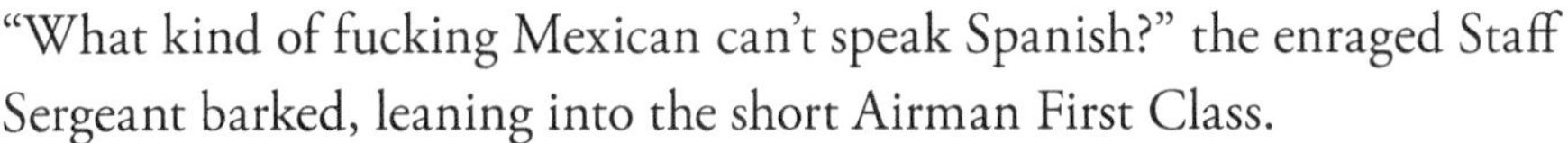

"What kind of fucking Mexican can't speak Spanish?" the enraged Staff Sergeant barked, leaning into the short Airman First Class.

"One from Chicago," Carlos Huerta replied. "I'm surprised you didn't know. Your wife sure does."

"Shut the fuck up and get on the aircraft, you fucking spic!"

Carlos shrugged, adjusted his gear, and climbed up the ladder into the cramped belly of the DC-3.

He sat in silence, wondering what the hell was going on, as did the rest of the enlisted Air Policemen stuffed into the lumbering bird. Some were headed to Korea. Carlos, among a few others, was returning from a twelve-month tour. All were armed—which was unusual. Carlos had a pump-action shotgun, even more unusual.

He wasn't the only one noticing the oddity. Every enlisted man on board was either Black or had a Spanish surname. About that time, Sergeant Jackson looked around and said, "Oh, fuck. Where the white boys?"

Heads swiveled. A wave of laughter followed.

"We're on the USS Expendable!" Carlos yelled.

"Or Shit Detail!"

"Or both," they all thought.

Two more transfers and countless hours later, Carlos was wheels-down somewhere in the desert. Which desert? Who knew. They were herded into a Quonset hut next to a set of hangars, grabbed bunks, and told to sleep.

The next day came debriefing: duration unknown, security clearance mandatory. Everyone signed a confidentiality agreement. Still no Asian or Caucasian enlisted men in sight.

Then the civilians arrived—almost all white. The tempo on base shifted. Activity picked up. An incoming "event" was expected.

Uniform name tags were removed. New, sterile identifiers were issued. Carlos became IDA98S.

One night, on patrol, Airman Rodriguez (IDA54S) from Los Angeles told Carlos he'd overheard a white civilian say, "Well, IT can read."

Two nights later, a fleet of massive cargo aircraft landed on the tarmac. The biggest Carlos had ever seen. Navy crews disembarked and began unloading huge, canvas-covered crates into the hangars.

Later that night, three rings of armed security were posted. Carlos was placed in the innermost ring, closest to the hangar. He was ordered to face *toward* it. Staggered twenty-five feet apart, behind sandbag walls, their orders were clear: use of deadly force authorized.

During his twelve-hour shifts, strange noises echoed from inside. Lights flickered. Aircraft came and went. Even after a year in a combat zone, Carlos had never seen activity like this.

Then came The Night.

A muffled pop from within the hangar. An alarm, quickly silenced. A gunshot. Total blackout.

Shapes moved. A scream.

The airman to Carlos's right shrieked—then flew through the air toward him. Carlos ducked. When he looked up, he saw it: a dark shape, blending with the air itself. It looked like fur but wasn't. Its red eyes floated seven feet off the ground.

Carlos fired. Two 00-buck rounds, center mass. The thing dropped.

Then he was flying. And then—nothing.

Ten days later, he woke up in the Naval Medical Center in San Diego. Coma. Blunt force trauma. A burn on his left bicep. Official story: fuel bladder explosion. When he asked about the creature, or the others, he was told:

"Shut the fuck up."

That night in October 1950 shaped Carlos M. Huerta for life.

He would chase the truth for decades. It would cost him three marriages and his relationship with two children. It would cost him half a lung, a full liver, and any chance at normalcy. Though several tobacco and liquor executives made fortunes off him.

He tried jobs. Many. None stuck.

In the late '70s, he met Shelly, a shy gal from Dallas who shared his obsession with government conspiracies. They met at a UFO conference in Cincinnati. She became wife number four. His favorite.

She never once told him to shut the fuck up.

In the spring of 1983, Shelly was struck by a car while on her bike. Two months later, Carlos snapped. He punched his boss and lit a stack of tires on fire.

Fired. Arrested. Skid Row.

The Holy Trinity.

Still, the pursuit continued. Every month, like clockwork, his mailbox overflowed: *UFO, The Unexplained, Fate, True, Paranormal Monthly, Popular Science, Popular Mechanics, Penthouse* (for the articles, of course), and fading stacks of mimeographed fanzines.

By the 2000s, Carlos moved via motorized wheelchair—not because his legs didn't work, but because lugging around his oxygen tank was a bitch. He scored a top-tier chair when a neighbor died. Slipped Doug, the maintenance man, a crisp fifty. Added a custom O2 holder and ashtray under the joystick.

Privilege.

There was no better sight than Senor Huerta, Art Carney's long-lost twin, holding court in the Baltimore lobby: white bucks, blue sweatpants, wife beater under one of a dozen bathrobes. Always topped with a brown bowler. Black-rimmed glasses. Oxygen in his nose.

Any new tenant got the treatment. A vending machine coffee (actually quite decent after monthly servicing), followed by a smile and a grilling.

"Sugar? Cream?"

He never broke eye contact.

"Former military?" he'd ask.

From there, every road led to: "You ever see something you couldn't explain?"

Some scoffed. Some remembered things in a haze of gin. But some said yes.

Carlos took notes. Drew maps. Connected dots.

Then he'd disappear upstairs to his fifth-floor lair. Days at a time. Once a week, he hit the Central Library. The librarians knew him well. They set aside anything about UFOs, Bigfoot, or government coverups.

Once, Mark offered to return some overdue books. Carlos invited him in.

Neat room. Books and magazines stacked with military precision. A desk. A typewriter. No photos of green goblins. No red yarn. Just order.

His room was like his mind. His interrogations: clean, efficient, and a little disarming.

He never stopped looking.

In his final months, he began calling into late-night AM shows using another tenant's internet radio hookup. He told his story again and again.

And then—he vanished.

Mark had been away for a couple weeks. When he returned, Carlos was gone. Room empty. Files gone. No one quite knew what happened.

Some say he gave a thirty-day notice. Others saw him being helped into a handicapped-accessible van. The next day, someone spotted him again— same guy, baseball cap, giant sunglasses (Carlos hated both), no oxygen tube in sight.

He watched as hired men from Home Depot loaded up his life into an unmarked van.

And like that, Carlos M. Huerta disappeared into Skid Row legend.

Mel-Mel

Melanie Rudisill finally found someone she could talk to without Leon threatening to kill her.

Leon was her boyfriend, sort of. They called him *Fightin' Leon* down at the King Eddy—he'd earned it, one bar scrap at a time. He was jealous, hot-headed, and the kind of man who clenched his fists when another guy so much as glanced her way. But for some reason, he never saw Mark— the morning bartender—as a threat. That worked just fine for Mel-Mel.

She needed someone to talk to. Skid Row wasn't exactly brimming with girlfriends. Most of the women were basket cases, in and out of psych wards or dead within the year. The men were drunks, junkies, or lazy old racists waiting on their next check. But the women? Mel-Mel said they came down here with actual defects—something broken in the wiring.

She liked to say things like that. She had a way of talking, like she was holding court at the end of the world. Her laugh came from the gut and sounded like it had gravel in it.

"He was sweet," she'd say about one ex, "but his addiction to kiddie porn? *Too grievous, baby.* Had to split."

Or:
"He used to buy me flowers, took me to movies, but one night I caught him humping my boot. My favorite boot, no less. *That*, my friend, was a grievous addiction to ladies' footwear."

She'd howl at that one. Mark always laughed too. Never knew what to say in return.

Melanie hit LA in 1974, straight off a Greyhound from Buffalo. She was 18 and terrified. The only contact she had was a guy named Al—grease monkey, long sideburns, used the word *bitchin'* like it was punctuation. She met him at a drag strip in Lancaster. He told her he surfed Malibu, and that was all she needed to hear.

When she called him from the downtown bus station, some guy with a leather coat and a big Afro tried to snatch her suitcase before she even finished dialing. Al answered on the second try. He didn't remember her. Then he did. Then he showed up.

They lived together in Sylmar for a while. She waitressed at Shakey's Pizza; he fixed cars and bought her a new recliner. Never did see him surf. But Melanie always had wanderlust—or maybe just a radar for chaos. One day she moved out and into the Hollywood apartment of one of her divorced-dad regulars. That led to years working the Strip: The Roxy, the Rainbow, even a stint as a Playboy Bunny. That ended with a three-way breakup involving another Bunny and the Bunny Mother, and, just like that, so did Mel-Mel's lesbian phase.

Decades passed in a blink. Nights blurred into mornings, faces into stories, stories into legend. One day Melanie looked in the mirror and realized she was on the wrong side of 40. The looks were gone. The charm was running on fumes. What was left was a busted liver, some bad teeth, and enough stories to fill a jukebox.

She lived off the pension of the only man she ever married—a half-Japanese rink tech who died on a Zamboni while cleaning the ice. It spun in circles for ten minutes before anyone noticed. They'd been married one year and one day. She only saw him twice that last month.

By the 2000s, Mel-Mel was living at the Baltimore Hotel. She liked it because the bars were close, the rent was cheap, and the old-timers left her alone. She met Leon at Cole's. He looked like a broken-down Santa Claus, but his face lit up when she talked. She liked that. She moved in not long after.

Leon had a temper but never laid a hand on her. He saved his punches for the barflies and bums who pushed their luck. Like the flasher on the sixth floor—a maybe-schizo in a tinfoil hat who used to be a stand-up comic on *The Tonight Show*, if the rumors were true.

That didn't surprise Melanie. She'd dated plenty of comics. Most of them were already wearing foil in their heads—just not on the outside.

In her last years, Mel-Mel told stories to anyone who'd listen, even if she'd already told them twice. It became part of her charm. Leon would drag her to the bar for a drink, and she'd find a new audience.

On a quiet Monday in 2010, Melanie Rudisill died in her recliner she'd hauled across LA since 1974. Al's old recliner.

She died mid-sentence, halfway through a story to an old friend.

Room 313

"The gods have abandoned 313—and so have I," said Doug the Viking, our fearless maintenance man and master of all New York Times crossword puzzles.

"The owner gave me the key—the only key. It's sequestered in a safe space, and I'd gladly lose all my fingernails through torture before I gave it up."

The three men stared at him in silence as he interrupted their paranormal conversation. Doug stood like a woodsman in court, hand on his mop handle, upright beside his rolling bucket, a noble peasant in worn-out overalls.

Charles leaned forward on the lobby counter, rolling his fifth cigarette. "I always wondered where that key was. Always wanted to check out that room. Just a look."

"Come on, Charles. You of all people know that's bullshit," Mark said, sipping his vending machine coffee.

"No, no," Dave Crazy cut in, "There's some weird stuff out there. I've seen it."

"Well, duh. You work in a mental institution."

Dave sighed deeply. "I've seen stuff here, man. And back home too. In Wisconsin, we've got this county road where people disappear."

"Now you sound like Carlos Huerta. Let's stick to ghosts."

Doug spoke up again, quieter this time. "About five years ago, I was changing the overhead light in 313. While I was up on the step ladder, the room got freezing cold—and the chair I brought in slid across the floor and slammed into the wall. Left scratches and a divot. I haven't been back since."

"See?" Dave said, nodding. "Remember when that plumber tried removing the radiator? Said the room got cold, something pulled his hair, and he heard whispering kids."

Charles nodded. "Freaked him out. Took off. Never came back."

"Such horseshit," Mark muttered.

Doug pushed past the clique, wheeling his mop into the lobby for his 3 a.m. cleaning shift.

"I've been here almost twenty years," Charles said, lighting his cigarette. "And before they locked it off, no one would stay in 313."

Right then, Young Ben walked in carrying two-gallon water jugs, casually crossing Doug's freshly mopped floor.

"Benjiman!" Doug snapped. "Did you not see the clean floor and my effort?"

Ben froze. "Oh. Sorry." He backed up perfectly, retracing each step, then pivoted and walked along the untouched edge.

"Well, I don't believe in any of that ghost crap," Mark said. "And Charlie, with your education, I'm surprised you do."

"What's horseshit?" Ben asked, slamming his jugs on the counter.

"313," Dave answered. "Mark says it's not haunted."

"Nah, it is. Victoria said she—"

Everyone groaned.

"What?" Ben protested. "She's been here longer than you assholes."

"I can't believe you fucked her," Mark said. "She's insane."

"She came on to me," Ben shot back. "Pushed me into her room."

"Okay, bring it down or I'll clear the lobby," said Charles.

We all laughed.

"Anyway," Ben continued, "Victoria said she saw the door breathing one night."

"Breathing?" Mark raised an eyebrow.

"Yeah. Expanding and contracting. Like it was taking a breath."

Dave nodded. "She told me that too."

"She heard voices," Charles said. "Kids crying."

"Has everybody gone nuts?"

"No," Ben said. "Just that Victoria's fucked everyone here but you."

More laughter.

"Whatever," Mark grumbled. "There's no such thing as ghosts. 313 is not haunted."

"I hate to break up your laugh fest," came a voice from the shadows. It was Willard, the retired engineer, crouched at the busted bookshelf. No one had seen him there.

"If Mark's so sure, why not test it? He spends the night in 313, gets the money we all throw in the kitty. Starting with my five bucks." He slapped it on the counter. "Unless he wants to give us odds."

"I'll match it," Mark said, standing tall.

Within minutes, residents came out of the woodwork. The kitty hit $220. Mark matched it.

"What about the key?" someone asked.

Twelve faces turned to Doug.

"For services rendered," he said solemnly, "I require fifteen percent of the full purse. In return, I'll produce the key."

"Okay," Mark said. "But rules. No one messes with me. No noises, no knocking, no wires. I'm checking the room top to bottom before I go in."

Agreed. The date: Friday the 13th.

For the next few days, Mark couldn't walk through the building without getting warned. Everyone had a story. More stories than residents.

In the 1950s, a down-on-their-luck couple supposedly slit each other's throats—then their kids'—in 313. Or maybe the mom did it and hung herself. Or maybe someone died peacefully in their sleep. Depends who was talking.

Even Victoria knocked on his door. Mark peeped through the hole and saw her, ranting as always. He slowly opened the door, half way.

Softly, she said: "Those demons will claw your eyes out while you sleep in there, you stupid, ugly man."

Then she walked off.

That Friday night, Mark arrived with a duffel bag and an audience. Strangely, the usual crew—Dave Crazy, Charles, Ben—weren't there. Mostly old timers now, a mix of doom and encouragement. Doug led him in.

"The gods be with you," he said, locking him inside.

The room was small. Peeling wallpaper. A busted radiator. One little window facing a brick wall. Mark plugged in his desk lamp, rolled out a sleeping bag, turned on the radio (surprisingly good reception), and cracked open *Salem's Lot*.

Hours passed. No ghosts. No voices. Just a cold, dusty room. Mark was actually starting to relax.

Then—BANG.

The door jumped in its frame. Mark flew against the far wall, dust coating him head to toe. He swung the door open just in time to catch a glimpse of Young Ben disappearing down the hall.

"Hey! Motherfuckers! We said none of that shit!"

"Just checking you were still alive," came Ben's voice from around the corner.

Mark closed the door and tried to not have a heart attack.

He woke up at 6:15 a.m., well-rested. Actually… better than usual.

Mark packed up, fantasizing about breakfast at the Monte Carlo diner across the street and how he'd spend that $400. A trip to Vegas? Some really good bourbon?

Ten minutes to go.

Then he heard voices outside. Spectators. Mark was touched.

Five minutes.

And that's when he made the decision he'd ponder for the rest of his life: He decided to play along. Why kill the story? Let the party live. He decided to be a star player in a long-term skid row legend

Doug knocked once.

When he opened the door, Mark bolted past him.

"Run! Dude, RUN!" He shouted.

Doug's face went pale. He slammed the door behind him and took off, both men racing past the stunned crowd. They screamed and scattered.

"I just want to get back to my room!" Mark shouted. "Don't ever open that door again!"

Once he made it back to his room, he nearly collapsed in laughter.

For days afterward, people kept asking, "What happened?" He gave them everything they wanted: levitating chairs, scratching from the ceiling, crying children.

"Why'd you stay, why didn't you leave?" they always asked.

He'd look them dead in the eye and say: "They wouldn't let me."

50 going on 20

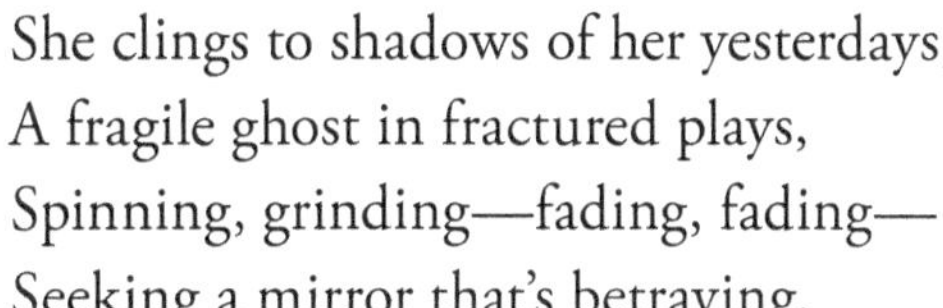

She clings to shadows of her yesterdays,
A fragile ghost in fractured plays,
Spinning, grinding—fading, fading—
Seeking a mirror that's betraying.

Her reflection, a stranger's face,
Lost in the hollow of her chase,
Strangers' approval—her fleeting crown,
A fleeting smile, a hollow sound.

She dances, disrobes, screams into the night,
A storm of noise, a desperate fight,
No one truly sees behind the mask—
Her silent cry, a hidden task.

Undone by youth's relentless tide,
Wrinkles claim what dreams have died,
Her last grind, her final dance,
A fleeting flicker in a hollow trance.

Smokeless joints, yet filled with haze,
A fog of pain that never fades,
Death approaches—inevitable, cold—
She settles for the pain she's told.

Hating what was, what might have been,
A shadow cast by what's unseen,
Her heart a prison, broken, torn—
Always chasing what's not form.

Buck Ass Naked

Athena walked carefully down the spacecraft's hallway, wary not to touch the fragile walls. Sensing danger, she slowed, crouched low, and raised her plasma blaster into the void.

SNAP!

A yellowish alien tentacle lashed out.

She fired.

SNAP!

Another tentacle grabbed her leg.

A third smacked her backward, launching her through the ship's cardboard wall, sending her prop blaster flying and smacking the Key Grip in the head.

"Goddammit!" he shouted.

"Cut!" came the director's voice, Kurt yelling from behind the giant monitor.

Crew scrambled onto the set, fixing walls and recovering the blaster, inspecting it for damage. Athena, buried under two rubber tentacles, called out.

"Hello? Can somebody help me up?"

"Kurt!" she finally screamed.

Kurt, balding and beer-bellied in a photographer's vest, ambled over.

"Sorry, babe. Hey Michael, James, help her up. C'mon folks!"

Two nervous PAs helped her up, careful not to touch anything lawsuit-worthy.

"Did ya get it? Want another?" she asked, brushing them off.

"Naw. If we do pickups, we'll get them before the space race scene Monday. You're wrapped for the day. Have a great weekend."

Athena's four favorite words: *wrapped for the day.*

An hour later, she was in her Honda Prelude with the sunroof open, flying down Burbank Blvd, blasting Motley Crue, watching the sun go down on a perfect California day.

She loved those drives—the freedom, the air, the feeling of being somebody.

She'd been in L.A. four years, ever since winning a bikini contest in Ann Arbor. First prize: a small role in a real Hollywood movie. No one told her the part involved a nude shower scene until the morning of the shoot.

Strangely, hitting her mark made her more nervous than standing *buck ass naked* in front of a camera crew. The other girls broke down, two had to be carried out drunk. Athena? She nailed it.

Alison Elizabeth Churchill was hooked.

She changed her name to Athena Conners—a tribute to the goddess and Chuck Connors from *The Rifleman.* She landed 34 more roles, mostly in low-budget sci-fi and horror, forever etched in late-night cable and VHS infamy.

The big studio jobs never came. One casting director chuckled after reviewing her early credits: Hooker #2, Lesbian Inmate #4, Titty Cop. From then on, it was B-movies or bust.

She danced at strip clubs along Sunset, took acting classes seriously, and eventually traded her thong for a bartending gig at a luxury hotel—after upgrading her breasts in '86. The new bust brought better parts, more dialogue, more screen time, and more of the expected nudity.

Athena was a true believer in craft. When asked why she still took classes despite being recognizable, she'd shrug: "We never stop learning, do we?"

By the late '80s, the money was good. She had a condo in Toluca Lake, access to better drugs, endless booze, and boyfriends with real record contracts.

She had rules. No drugs during work weeks. No coke before sex—kept the ol' "cocaine cock" situation in check. She liked her rockers cocked, locked, and loaded.

Then came the '90s. Younger actresses with tighter everything started landing the lead roles in an evolving low-budget scene. Sci-fi and horror flicks with rubber monsters gave way to softcore thrillers with moody jazz and sultry detectives.

So, Athena upgraded the breasts again, got a gym membership, and skipped the Strip—both boulevard and tease. But the work kept drying up.

Fan conventions became her lifeline.

Armed with autographed VHS tapes, new headshots, and knockoff merch, she hit the circuit. The fans were generous, especially the late-twenty-somethings who'd grown up watching her movies. The money wasn't huge, but it was consistent.

She once returned to Ann Arbor for a radio-sponsored hometown hero event—the same station that had launched her Hollywood dream. The parade, the speeches, the adoring fans—it felt good. She posed with her old high school cheerleading squad, proud to be the only one not shaped like a refrigerator.

What they didn't know: she'd had to spend a weekend in Palm Springs with the radio station's married owner and his girlfriend to get the gig.

Sex had always been transactional, even when it wasn't for a role. She picked men based on looks, hoping they were either well-endowed or knew what to do with their hands. Most failed. When she wanted a part, she slept with who she had to. Saved time.

So, when a fan offered $5,000 for a night, she paused… then said, "Sure, baby. When and where?"

She left his hotel room richer, but uneasy. She told herself she'd done more for less. But this was different. Cleaner. Direct.

She was now, officially, a prostitute.

Back at her hotel, she raided the minibar to calm the nerves. The slope was slippery, and she was already sliding.

The gigs increased. Word got around. The internet, she claimed later, ruined everything—made her "side hustle" known to just the right (or wrong) people. She was approached more by couples than men, and her rates floated, depending on desperation.

The IRS didn't know. Neither did her agent, Stuart. That worked—until it didn't.

In the late '90s, Athena got caught in a prostitution sting out of state. The details were always hazy in her retellings. But the story followed the usual arc: arrested, fired, Skid Row. The Holy Trinity.

She sold the condo to fund her legal battle. Stuart sued for his 15% of "everything." The IRS wanted their share, too.

In the end, Athena was sentenced to seven years. She served three years and change.

When she got out, broken in spirit and body, she returned to L.A. Her only asset: a friend who let her crash… until they gave her the boot.

She worked as a cleaner for a trucking company, and lived in Skid Row SROs. Her eyesight made driving a challenge. She clung to men who offered alcohol and a roof.

One of them was Paulie, a former paralegal battling a crack addiction. He treated her right, even when she didn't deserve it. She cheated, drank, flirted—he stayed, for a while.

He left, got clean, got a job. She moved in with a neighbor—the same one she'd been cheating with. That lasted a few months. He kicked her out, saying, "The room's too small for two big egos."

By 2010, she was pushing 50. Off parole. Still beautiful, in a worn, world-weary way.

She borrowed $500 from her old roommate and took a bus to Texas. Found a kind woman at AA, moved in, and together they opened a kids' indoor bounce gym.

Athena found peace. She found purpose. She never looked in the mirror.

Well, except for that $500. She still hasn't paid it back.

Not that anyone's surprised.

Nice and Still

Nice and still.
That's how you have to be after you break into a car you're about to
steal.

Ivan sat still behind the wheel of a 2003 black-on-black Lexus sedan.
No car alarm. That was weird.
Maybe this model had a recall coming down the line, some computer
bug. For now, it was a blessing.

He hated boosting Lexuses. Or Audis. Or Caddies. Especially Benzes.
Not because they were hard—he could handle hard—but because they
were hard to move unless someone pre-ordered them. But tonight?
Tonight was one of those rare orders.

Some fool wanted a 2003 black-on-black Lexus, no substitutions.
Ivan paid a homie at the DMV a hundred bucks for a list.
This one was number twelve out of seventeen.

Quiet street. No dogs. No looky-loos.
Gotta love the Westside.

He broke the ignition and wheel lock. Jammed a flathead into the
column and turned it slow.
The motor gave a soft, satisfied purr.

He reached into the backseat, slid his tools under the floor mat, then
eased the car into gear.
Clean. Almost too clean.

Then he saw it.

OnStar.

"Fuck," he muttered. "Fucking Lexus."

He drove another mile, found an empty side street, popped the hood, and hit it with his penlight. Located the black box near the master brake cylinder, cracked it open, yanked two fuses.
Waited.

No sputter. No hiccup.

Clean again.

He slammed the hood and got back in.
"Sun Valley, here we come."

The ride was smooth—no cops, no traffic, no radio chatter.
Just dark roads and the soft hum of a stolen car.

At 2:00 AM sharp, he rolled into Ernesto's junkyard.
Next door, the tranny club was still going, freaks spilling out onto the sidewalk, smoking, fighting, grinding to muffled reggaeton.

God doesn't always frown on the wicked.

As Ivan idled, a tall she-he in a too-tight dress tapped on his window.
He didn't roll it down, just shook his head and glared.

She threw up her hands and walked off.
Ivan caught a glimpse of her ass in the streetlight—tight, high. Not bad.
He thought, for half a second, about a quick blowjob.
After all the time he did inside, it wasn't the biggest leap. But the garage door started to rise.

He pulled in. Just as the back bumper cleared, the door slammed shut behind him like a guillotine.

Ernesto stepped out of the shadows.

"Well, if it ain't our favorite Dominican."

They shook hands. Ernesto was 6'3", but he looked like a stick next to Ivan—5'7" and built like a powerlifter carved out of mahogany.

Ivan liked to say all the men—and some of the women—in Santo Domingo looked like him. Always got a laugh.

"You got my cash?" he said.

Ernesto held up his hands. "OnStar?"

Ivan smiled, held up the two fuses.

Behind them, Ernesto's crew tore into the Lexus—scraping VINs, gutting electronics, making the car disappear. Two hours, tops.

By sunrise, Ivan was back in his room at the Baltimore Hotel in Downtown LA.

He hated that place.

Drunk old gringos reeking of piss and mothballs glaring at him like he didn't belong. He'd love to throw hands, but parole kept him grounded. A few of them were cool, though.

Doug the maintenance guy—skinny white dude with a weird accent who never slept.
He was good for weed, once Ivan got him to stop charging "white folk prices."
And the bartender across the street at King Eddy's.
Ivan could never remember his name, called him "Buddy." Doug called him "Dynamite," for some weird whiteboy reason.
The guy also worked at a strip club as a bouncer.
Ivan told him he had that machete-killer look—the kind of face that doesn't flinch. The bartender just nodded and changed the subject to pussy.

Ivan liked Victoria, too.
A forty-something Mexican lady who roamed the halls in thrift store gowns, babbling in gibberish. Most men avoided her. Some lured her into their rooms.
But whenever she saw Ivan, she'd stop, place her hand on her chest, and say in perfect Castilian:

"Hello Ivan. I hope your day is blessed."

Then back to the gibberish.

Back in his room on the sixth floor, Ivan lay on his mattress watching sunbeams poke through the holes in his curtain.
He'd just made five grand.
And he still had to live in this dump.
Still couldn't own a car.
Still had to clock in at the flower market for $8 an hour.

Two more years of this shit until parole ended.

He fell asleep to the sound of the city waking up.

A few weeks later, Ivan was in the lobby cooling off before heading upstairs when a girl came bouncing down the stairs.

Short, thick, wearing a red sweater tight enough to be considered a threat. She asked for change from Terry, the desk clerk Ivan didn't like. He moved in with his best smile.

"Girl, you're gonna need more than spare change to take *me* out. I'm expensive."

She didn't even blink.

"Get outta my way, fool. I ain't got time for you."

She pushed past him and hit the vending machines.
He followed like a stray mutt.

Her name was Ingrid.
Eighteen, came to care for her uncle Gus after his heart attack.
Ivan kept at her—catcalls, jokes, gifts.
Finally, he stole a Miata convertible and offered her a ride home.

That sealed the deal.

Within three weeks, Ingrid moved into Ivan's room.
By week seven, the fights started.

She was young, fiery, and smart. Ivan was possessive, hot-tempered, paranoid.

He didn't like her talking to other men.
She didn't like being controlled.

They denied ever throwing the first punch.
But the first punch *was* thrown—and after that, the clock started ticking.

Somehow, they avoided the police. Until they didn't.

One Saturday night, voices escalated.

> "Don't talk to no one! Go to the market, get the food, and come back. Don't talk to *nobody*, hear me?"

> "Why you act like this? I love you, baby. I'd *die* for you."

> "Die for me?"

And with that, Ivan threw open the window, climbed out, and hung from the sash.

Just his fingers gripping the ledge, sixty feet up.

> "I'm not *talking*, bitch! I'm *showing*! Stop talking to everybody!"

> "Okay! Okay! Baby, come back in!"

Ivan tried to pull himself up.
Couldn't.

His feet scrabbled against the wall—no grip.
His arms were gassed. Panic set in.

Ingrid screamed, tried to pull him up, but she couldn't.
People started to gather below.

Two minutes passed. Felt like two hours.
His fingers began to give.

Then—

BANG!

The door flew open, kicked in from the outside.

The bartender—Mark—rushed to the window, grabbed Ivan under the arms, braced his knee against the wall, and heaved.

"I got you, dude. I ain't letting you go."

It took everything, but inch by inch, he pulled Ivan back inside.

They collapsed on the floor. Ingrid sobbed on the bed.

"What the fuck happened, Ivan? Y'all good?" Mark asked.

Ivan tried to speak, but outside, a fire truck wailed.
It paused, conferred with the crowd, then rolled off, back to the station and "America's Got Talent."

"I was cleaning the window," Ivan said awkwardly.

"Alright," Mark nodded. "Just be careful, man."

He turned to leave.

"Sorry about your door."

"I got it," Ivan muttered. "Thanks buddy."

Ingrid lay her head in his lap.

"That guy saved your life; his name is Mark" she whispered.

"Shut up," Ivan said.

A month later, Ingrid left.

He'd slapped her in the stairwell. She didn't wait around.

She went to Jalisco, Mexico—back to her family.

Ivan followed.

In a town he couldn't pronounce, outside a bar called The Bali Room, Ivan picked a fight with two local men.

He squared up, ready.

Then—**crack**—a flash behind his head.
A pinpoint sting.
He tried to move, but his body wouldn't answer.

His knees buckled. He dropped straight down like a puppet with cut strings.

Flat on his back, looking up.

The samba still thumped from the bar.
His vision dimmed. Blackness spread like water in ink.

Then—two tiny white lights, dead center.
They grew, expanding into a tunnel.

And he saw his grandfather, Oswaldo, slicing a mango with dirty hands and smiling.
His grandmother fussed at him for feeding the baby without washing.
Ivan could smell the fruit. Could feel the sticky pulp on his fingers.

Warmth flooded his chest.

For the first time in years, Ivan felt…

Nice and still.

Night of the Ninja(s)

Great moments in humanity can always begin with a decision—no matter how insane or calculated—the decision to say yes. To gather and rise in the affirmative.

It's one of the bottlenecks in history, if you will.

Like the last stand of the 300 Spartans against the Persian Empire, which led to the birth of Western culture.

Like the building of the John Browning Toll Road, which led to the birth of Los Angeles. (Calling it John Brown was such a gangster move back then. I remember being a very young boy on my great-grandpa's farm, deep in the South, and listening to his 95-year-old neighbor, Mr. Dawson—a man who knew slaves—shout out "John Brown!" as a cuss word after he sampled some of my Uncle Pate's moonshine, when his fourth wife Ella wasn't around.)

Like when Stanislav Petrov, a Soviet Air Defense officer, ignored his control panel that screamed at him that the Yankee Capitalist Pigs had just launched half a dozen nuclear missiles. Instead of launching a retaliation strike and giving the world a nuclear enema, he chilled, convinced it was a typical Soviet tech malfunction. Thanks, Stanny.

So, it was on a forgotten day in July of 2005 that I said yes to installing an illegal and dangerous digital reception device on the roof of the Baltimore Hotel. All in the name of cultural access.

I wanted PBS. I needed ninjas and engineers. What I got was Dave Crazy and Willard.

First, I tried Viking Doug, the maintenance man.

"Fuck no and don't ask me again," Doug snapped. "Five antenna rigs are up. Any more and I get in trouble."

"C'mon, Doug. I'll give ya fifty bucks to look the other way."

"Dynamite, I know you're going to try. I will stop you, and I will report you to Bob Rhollings."

Bob Rhollings: the building manager, racist jackass, and champion of evictions. Bob hated two things: Black folks and Charlie, the nighttime desk clerk. I was friends with both. My only saving graces:

1. I paid my rent on time.
2. I kept to myself.

Down on the Skid, that was currency.

"Doug, I only get one channel—and that's on a good day."

"Good luck. May the gods smile upon you," he said, walking off.

Why Dave Crazy? Not because he was crazy—he worked as a monitor at a mental hospital. He'd wrestle down a McMurphy by day, then come home to his neighbors, many just as unstable but better armed.

Dave had a shaved head, gray goatee, gapped teeth, and wild eyes. A fellow ninja.

Willard looked like what he was: an engineer. Late 60s, pleated jeans, zippered half-boots, and perfectly ironed shirts. He moved and spoke with mathematical efficiency. His daughter tried every month to get him out of the Baltimore. He never budged.

Rumor had it he once stripped down and masturbated on his drafting table at work while listening to The Go-Go's. Fired. Arrested. Skid Row. The holy pipeline.

Last year, he showed me a schematic for a system that would alert residents when their laundry was done. It would've costed the building $195. Bob Rhollings laughed in his face.

Willard had been looking for payback ever since.

"Mark, I can rig up an antenna disguised as a rain gutter. Parts: twenty-one bucks. Labor: free. You'll need fifty feet of coax."

"What's your favorite Go-Go's song?", I asked.

"Vacation"

My guy.

Dave and I had been on the roof plenty, until 2003, when they locked it down. Cameras. Alarms. If caught, you'd be arrested and banned, gift-wrapped by Bob Rhollings.

We plotted while Willard built our rig.

There were four ways onto the roof:

1. Fire escape (West)
2. Fire escape (East)
3. Stairwell
4. Elevator

The East fire escape had a clear view from Gomez's window—Bob's informant. So East was out.

West? That was Oklahoma Bob's room. Former cowboy stuntman, now battling Huntington's. I once helped him during a seizure. After I got him his meds, he looked at me and asked:

"Mark, do I scare you?"

"No, Bob. Not you."

"You know a man's old when no one sees him as a threat anymore."

The paramedics arrived and greeted Bob warmly; he was a good customer.

He agreed to help. "If I see you go past my window, I'll wave. Good luck with those cameras."

Stairwell? Alarm and full camera coverage. No go.

The elevator? Now that had promise.

I'd learned its secrets after being trapped inside with a crackhead. Firefighters had to manually raise it from the motor room above. No cameras up there. I also watched them open the door with a slender tool that dropped an L-shaped paddle through a hole.

I described it to Willard. The next day, he handed me a perfect replica. And some red Solo cups.

"Cups?" Dave asked.

"Stick them over the cameras from behind. They'll know someone was up there, but not who."

The antenna was a work of art: aluminum flashing with copper webbing, grounding wires on one end, coax on the other.

"What do I do with this?" I asked.

He handed me a hand-drawn schematic with installation notes, then explained it like we were third graders—which wasn't far off.

Night of the Ninja. PBS, here I come.

It was midnight. Cool LA air, stars out. We sent the elevator to Five. Willard opened the door. I stepped onto the roof of the cab. Dave joined me, antenna in hand. My backpack held the rest.

We nodded. Willard called it: "I'll enter the cab and hold it until you signal. Tap when you're clear."

The door shut. Then, suddenly, we dropped.

Someone had called the elevator.

The cab fell. Fast. Victoria, the building lunatic, had summoned it from the third floor.

Cables screamed. Dave looked at me with eyes that said: *"If I survive this, I'm going to kill you."*

The doors opened. Victoria babbled all the way down to the lobby. The doors shut. Willard hit 6.

"You two still there?"

"Go, man!"

The ride up was worse. The ceiling rushed at us. Just when I thought we'd be crushed—we stopped.

We climbed off the cab into the motor room. I tapped. Willard left.

The roof was ours.

It was perfect. Quiet. Clear. Beautiful.

Dave dropped the coax down to my window, then his below mine. He taped the wire down. I installed the antenna, wired it to the floodlight housing. No sparks. No drama.

Done in twenty-five minutes. Ninja work. We beamed.

"It's art," Dave whispered.

Then: *PING.* The elevator door opened.

Someone had used a key that only Bob Rhollings possessed.

"Go," I said. "I'll grab the tools."

Dave dashed to the fire escape. I shouted, "Don't forget the cameras!"

He slapped cups on the lenses from behind and vanished.

Bob waved him into his window. Bob motioned to the cracked door. They saw Doug and security guard Melvin at the bottom of the stairs.

The jig was up.

I was halfway across the roof when I saw Melvin open the stairwell door.

"LAPD! Stop!" from behind me.

I stopped.

The ride to the lobby was quiet. I was cuffed. Tools in a bag: wire stripper, Phillips head, camera.

Doug caught my eye. "Dynamite, I am not the author of this. King Edward's manager saw you while partaking in a smoke break on their roof. Called Rhollings. This I promise."

I nodded.

Oklahoma Bob spoke with the cops. They listened.

"What do you want him charged with?" the officer asked Rhollings.

"Trespassing! I want him out!"

"No trespass. No vandalism. If you want to evict, use the sheriff. He's a legal tenant."

They uncuffed me.

"You're outta here, fuckhead!" Rhollings barked.

"Let me know when the sheriff gets here," I said.

He stormed off.

I turned to Oklahoma Bob

"Bob, what did you tell them?"

"Aw, son. Cops love a cowboy."

Epilogue:

A flirty call to the owner's secretary later, Rhollings was leashed again.

Dave and I had perfect reception. Seven crisp channels. Even PBS.

One week later, I saw Doug putting up a flyer:

"Make an appointment to install your satellite dish."

"Doug, what the hell?"

"Wanted to see if you would attempt it, Dynamite," he laughed.

"The gods work in mysterious ways," I muttered.

Doug laughed harder than I'd ever seen.

Just Some White Guy

Ass kicker. Shot Caller. Ramrod. Top Dog. Chief. Hoss. Whatever you call him, every crew has one—the man in charge. Doesn't matter if you're drilling oil, pouring concrete, or running a glory hole peep show in downtown L.A., the top guy always has one thing in common:

He's a fucking asshole.

Robert Cezary Rhollings was no exception.

He left the Marine Corps in the winter of '73 after three tours in Vietnam. Came home to Jackowo, Chicago—still a Polish kid with a short fuse and a taste for tequila. After twenty minutes on his parents' couch, he kissed his mom, patted his drunk dad's shoulder, and split. He boarded a train to Portland with $800 from the sale of his '65 Panhead— something he'd mourn till his dying day.

He lasted six months on a linen truck before getting canned for drinking on the job. The next few years, he bounced between construction sites, bottle in hand. Married a bartender named Patsy. They had a kid. Gave it up for adoption "as a mercy," he'd later say. Came home once to find Patsy in bed with three Black men. He sent two to the hospital and went to jail for the third because he used a sock full of nickels.

From '79 to '85, Bob was arrested 27 times. Public drunk. Assault. Bad checks. San Francisco denied him a printing job after that last one.

By the mid-'80s, he'd settled in North Beach, managing an adult theater. Married a Greek woman named Davina who tried to kill him three times—twice in his sleep, once with a shotgun. She missed and landed in jail. He took over her flophouse when the IRS seized it, dodging jail by pinning the fraud on her and her "shadowy" family.

He blew town and showed up in L.A. in 1990, working at a porno booth downtown. His job? Mop up semen, fix token machines, and chase off sex workers. He hated humanity and let everyone know it by offering up beatings to bums, drunks, perverts, hookers, and pimps, who made him work above his paygrade.

He drank away his days at the King Eddy, scowling into his glass.

Then he met Bill Stallings, a like-minded saloon keeper, who introduced Bob to the new owner of the Baltimore Hotel.

By winter of '92, Bob was the assistant manager. He ran the day shift and decided who got a room. Requirements? Whatever Bob said they were. Mostly, the place was old white guys on pensions drinking their checks across the street. A kingdom of has-beens and hangovers.

Soon Bob was top dog. The Hoss. The Big Guy. The Top. He called himself "Top Asshole." That fit. He let women in if there were favors involved. Kept a roster of stoolies and favorites. Kicked people out for infractions real or imagined. Especially if they were Black.

One of his best friends was Bob Morgan— "Biltmore Bob"—a former paratrooper turned doorman at the fancy hotel five blocks west. They were opposites. Rhollings was loud, aggressive, average-looking, with the kind of face that beat three police lineups. Witnesses always wrote: "Just some white guy."

Biltmore Bob was tall, soft-spoken, with haunted blue eyes and the same military buzzcut he'd had since '64. He got a job at the luxury hotel after working as a body guard for a Lebanese drug dealer who met his fate in the night waters off the coast of Acapulco.

This did not happen on Biltmore Bob's watch.

The two Bobs became inseparable. They drank, laughed, and ruled the lobby from behind a pair of tall chairs.

Bob Rhollings had enemies too. Chief among them: Charles Luke, the night clerk. Educated, principled, and unafraid to challenge Bob's reign. Tensions exploded when Charles gave a coveted sixth-floor room to a former bartender named Mark—someone Bob couldn't intimidate. Mark was trouble. Hooked up with residents' wives, dropped acid and roamed the hallways taking pictures with an empty camera, and he was a prime suspect in a porno filmed in the basement. Bob hated him.

Bob retaliated by framing Charles for theft. Got him fired. But Charles fought back, got a settlement, and a room at the King Edward across the street.

Bob got fired.

He left with a black woman named Sharla to live on a commune up north. Years later, when Biltmore Bob was dying, Rhollings came back—older, softer, broke. He moved into Bob's room to care for him. Handled his checks. Called the shots.

Until Shelly—Bob's wife—took control of the finances.

Now jobless, broke, and over sixty, Rhollings had nowhere to go. The hotel had new owners. They were gutting rooms. Making plans.

Then one day, the sheriff kicked in the door.

They found Bob curled up in the closet, five days dead. Needle still in his arm. His first- and last-time trying heroin.

The bedbugs had already claimed the body.

As they carried him out past the cracked lobby tile, no one said his name. No one remembered the Hoss, the Top, the Asshole King of the Baltimore.

They just said:

"Who was that?"

"Just some white guy."

D.S. Nutes

Doug the Viking—or Viking Doug, or D. S. Nutes, as the coroner would be told—checked into the afterlife under a joke name written on a room card. Even in death, Doug played the enigma part to the end. D. S. Nutes. A pun, a riddle, a smirk.

He was the maintenance man for the Baltimore Hotel, and also for the King Edward across the way when both buildings shared the same elusive owner. Not many people knew much about Doug—and Doug wasn't about to let anyone get close enough to find anything out.

Mister Nutes stood six-foot-three. The day after Thanksgiving, soaked in a wet parka, he might've weighed 125 pounds. His skin was a pale pink-white, vacuum-sealed around his skeleton like shrink-wrap over frozen beef.

He wore the same thing every day: an old t-shirt (size extra small, still billowed), overalls with sagging front pockets stuffed with Marlboros, a rusted zipper, and a baggie of some of the finest kind bud east of the 405. Shoes varied—either barefoot or in a pair of brown Crocs, depending on the weather and mood.

He had long white hair and a beard to match, never trimmed, never brushed, just a living totem of some forgotten tribe. He spoke slowly, with precision. A dry, brilliant cadence that made him sound like a southern professor stripped of the drawl.

In his downtime—when he decided it was downtime—he could be found in the Literature section of the downtown public library, reading but never borrowing. Or on the roof, smoking weed and talking to himself in a philosophical hush.

No one really knew where he came from. Rumor said one of the Dakotas, and somehow it mattered which one. Some claimed he'd been a friend of the building's owner and arrived with him in the early '90s. Others swore they'd seen him wandering the halls long before that. His origin was fogged in by guesses and half-tales. His response to any inquiry: "It does not matter. I am not that interesting."

Which, of course, made him interesting as hell.

He knew motors—especially the two-wheeled kind—and once gave his reason for never flying: "I have obtained so much surgical steel, not only do I set off the detectors, they have to seat me carefully, or I'll unbalance the plane."

He had three tattoos; black India ink symbols whose meanings were never explained. They hinted at prison time, as did the cratered scars along the insides of his arms. He never spoke about them. He didn't have to.

He was never seen eating. Occasionally he'd return from the Fifth Street market with a paper sack of groceries, but no one saw the food go in, and no one saw the trash come out.

His age was a moving target. Outside in daylight, he looked well over 70. In the low-wattage shadows of the laundry room, he could pass for a man in his thirties. Something about Doug bent time.

He worked when he felt like it. And when he worked, things got fixed—quietly, perfectly, and without instruction. If something needed doing and it was permitted, he'd handle it. If it wasn't? You'd be told to pound sand, in the most dignified tone imaginable.

He was one of the few people invited into Carlos Huerta's room, the Baltimore's resident conspiracy theorist. They'd talk for hours. No one knew about what.

Doug was paid in cash—every Friday, in an envelope. The only staff member on the books that way. He had no phone, no email, no credit score. No bills. No footprint.

He lived in a tiny room tucked beneath the roof-access stairwell on the sixth floor. Quiet. Unbothered. Unreachable. And not the type to be running from anything—though he had the vibe of a man who had outrun everything that ever tried to catch him.

At one point, a curious resident working part-time for a detective agency tried to "solve the Viking." All roads were dead ends. Fingerprints were considered. But in the end, he let it go—out of respect, maybe. Or fear. Or the understanding that some people aren't meant to be known.

Doug the Viking, D.S. Nutes was found dead in his bed, two days after anyone last saw him. Heroin overdose. Needle still in his arm. Quiet and alone, the way he lived.

Out of respect, the staff told the police he was a resident. Just a guy who misplaced his ID. The name on his card: D. S. Nutes.

The cops got the joke.

And we all laughed too. Because it was perfect.

David

You start your morning by screaming Yiddish obscenities out your 6th-floor window for exactly four minutes. Some of your neighbors time you.

You pace, trying to figure out what went wrong yesterday and how *they* almost got you. You've worn an uppercase "L" into the linoleum from all the pacing. You didn't notice it until a neighbor pointed it out. You still believe it was already there when you moved in 15 years ago.

It's Tuesday. Grocery day.

You peek through your door to get a proper read on the Waves and how strong they are. Tuesdays are generally low. The folks at the Station do bookwork on Tuesdays—they're lazy cattle. Other, more important tasks go under the radar.

You time the door openings. Repetition is key. Always 3 to 6 times— never more than 6. Five is best. A number the Nazis hate.

Four door openings. At least five inches each. The Waves are super low. Maybe the supervisors at the Station are chewing out the cattle, so no one's directing the Waves today.

You ready yourself for the journey. Getting to the bus is the most dangerous part. Once you're on, the Waves can't reach you, and the other cattle usually leave you alone.

The elevator groans into motion—nope. Stairs today.

You run down six flights like a ten-year-old, bounding, skipping steps, vaulting handrails, you really enjoy this. Both fists under your chin like a gangly boxer, you burst through the lobby and out onto the sidewalk.

Time to blend in. Slow the walk. Lower the fists.

You kill time re-running conversations from years ago—ones that didn't go your way. You fix them in your head now, saying the right things, clearing up confusion. Sometimes you mutter these fixes aloud. Some of the cattle give you looks. Can't be helped. These things must be sorted.

Seated on the bus, the little Waves bounce off the metal shell. Even with the cattle using their personal brain cell destroyers to play games or holding them to their ears to babble nonsense, the steel protects you.

You rest easy. Go over a few more conversations.

Your stop approaches: Pico and Doheny.

Getting off, the cattle make remarks about your smell. But they're the ones who stink—chemical-scrubbed and factory-washed. You smell like nature. They've forgotten what that is.

Blocking out their offensive smells is easy. Like turning down a volume knob in your brain.

Three blocks later, you spot your deli. It's been there since the '70s. You lived nearby once. Dated a Persian girl with a flat stomach. You used to rest your head on her belly while she combed your hair and told you to shave, classical music playing on the radio.

She wouldn't recognize you now. Your beard brushes your chest.

Time to let the deli owners know you're there. They probably already know. It's Tuesday.

You pace in front of the deli door five times. Then you go around to the back alley.

Two Mexican workers sit on milk crates, smoking. You recognize them but avoid eye contact. That's how *they* get in—through the eyes. One tried to talk to you 12 years ago. It was all you could do not to scream, "You're making yourself a conduit!"

The back door opens. The owner appears with a gallon of water and a plastic bag of groceries. You do him the great courtesy of not looking in his eyes. You snatch the bag and nod deeply. He sees only the slightest tilt of your chin. He's used to it now.

You catch the Pico bus back downtown. You can't test the Waves again. Too risky.

The bus pass came from your brother. Each month, an envelope appears in your mailbox behind the front desk—pass and fifty bucks. He used to try to hand it to you in person. Used to beg you to come home. He's a doctor. You won't make him a target. Nazis only like their own kind to be doctors.

You've tried to explain the service you're doing for him. He won't listen. No one does.

You file those conversations away. More to sort.

Outside your building, you don't pace anymore. Instead, you sway, burp, and stare at the elevator door for four minutes. It clears the Waves. Neighbors still time you.

The lobby empties. You rush inside, press the elevator key with your brass skeleton key. Germ-free.

Germs aren't what they used to be. Back in the day, they ran your life. All because of that safety video you had to watch at the restaurant job—the one that explained, in microscopic detail, how germs infest everything. That week, you didn't sleep. Washed your hands, clothes, and sheets until your fingers bled.

But over time, the germs gave way to the Waves. The real threat.

Now, you're a hard target. Study, attack, confrontation, assimilation—you resist it all.

The bag has deli meats, hummus, cheeses, and a loaf of fresh rye. Kosher. Even the water.

You used to drink more than a gallon a week. Now, you use a trick. Fill the measuring cup from cough syrup to the first line. Add that to a glass of faucet water. It purifies instantly.

The trick is getting it to the *exact* line. Table must be level. You tap it to release bubbles. If it's off? Start over.

The water always tastes remarkable.

Sun sets. City noise swells. Night crews arrive at the Stations. Veterans and they are wiley. They focus on the Waves. If you go out—maybe to the Store or a peep booth in Hollywood—you'll need to be ready. Might need protection under the hat.

White vans will be out. Not as bad as weekends, but there'll be abductions.

Don't be one of them.

Midnight. You have to go out.

You test the door. The Waves are high. Pacing begins. Back and forth on the "L."

The urge to go is overwhelming. It wins.

You mold foil around your skull, tight and snug. Bucket hat over the top. Extra shielding.

Cool night. Helps with the sweat.

You take a different bus. Ride it all the way to Sunset and King. You don't need to look. You just *know* when you're there.

Walk west. Past the Riot House. Remember the parties—real rock 'n' roll mayhem. You were part of it. When you were still impure. Still cattle.

There it is. The Comedy Store.

You shake, every time.

You remember 1977. First time on stage. Nervous but focused. Later, bigger sets. Robin Williams bought you drinks. Did lines with you in the hallway. Joked about your nose. Everyone laughed.

The Store got you on the Tonight Show. You crushed. Johnny Carson brought you to the couch. You killed with a Hebrew school joke. Your mom called the next day—crying with pride.

That was before the Nazis came for you.

You warned people. No one listened. Too complex for their small, normal lives.

Cops came. Cuffs slapped on. You fought. Always outnumbered.

You pass the doorman. He pretends not to see you.

You find the booker. First eye contact of the day. Brutal, but necessary.

He has a 2:15 slot. Small room.

You nod.

You spot Don. Always has good weed.

You make your approach. "Excuse me, Don. Do you have any pot? May I make a purchase?"

He nods. You follow him out back.

He lights one for you.

Warm, syrupy calm. The city lights glow like stained glass. The Waves melt away.

2:15. Showtime.

The crowd is small. Mostly jacked-up comics with nowhere else to go. One of them—nobody likes him—hands out flashlights and lasers. Halfway into your set, they start beaming lights into your eyes. The lasers are the worst.

You forget your place.

You do stand-up because it's the last piece of your mother's smile. You're not the man who sat on Carson's couch. But few awakened ones are.

You float among the cattle.

You leave the stage fast. Catch the eastbound bus just in time.

Alone. Adjusting your gear. Shaking lights from your retina.

The city passes.

You remember Lacy from Florida. Massaging your feet, high as a kite, telling stories from the Universal Studios gift shop.

The bus driver watches you carefully.

But that's fine.

The Waves got him long ago.

Oklahoma Bob

Bob Quigley didn't care for heights. Never did.
Said a man ought not exceed the height of a saddle horn.

But nobody ever cared what Bob cared for.
Not the Big Bug on the ranch he worked as a boy.
Not the Marine drill instructors.
And certainly not the four Korean soldiers he had to stick with his bayonet just this side of the Chosin Reservoir.

But here he was—standing tall on a saloon roof, looking down at a film crew looking up at him.

He took a deep breath and waited for his cue: the fourth gunshot fired from the so-called hero of the picture—a star who could barely ride a horse and had a habit of punching stuntmen during movie fights.

Bob had to wait for his cue, drop his rubber pistol *away* from the landing pad, and *most importantly*, keep it out of the camera frame.

Behind him, out of the shot, was his soon-to-be best friend, Hardtack Delmonte—a fellow Korean War vet. Army paratrooper. Saddle tramp. Said he was from "a place in Texas where Houston is way up north."

   "How ya doin', Bobby?" Hardtack whispered.
   "I'm as ready as I was ten minutes ago."

Hardtack noticed Bob's legs starting to tremble.

   "I'll tell ya what, Bob… I bet the holdup's Number One's horse.
She can smell a queer a mile away—let alone sittin' on top of her."

Bob nearly busted a gut holding back a laugh. His legs steadied.

A crackle from the bullhorn broke up the rooftop duo's fun.

"Hey Bob, you ready?" the DA called from 29 and a half feet below.
"Ready!" Hardtack shouted back.
"Rolling! Speed... and action!"

Bob's mind went crystal clear.
Fear and hesitation were visiting someone else.

He focused on the landing pad below and pointed his gun at the hero, who was barely controlling his horse.

Hardtack counted out the gunshots.

"...Three... Four... Go, Bobby!"

Bob reacted to being shot, leaned forward, spotted his mark, and fell headfirst into the hot summer air.

On the way down, he found time to reminisce.
Jumping into Crystal Creek back home in Sedee, Oklahoma, on summer days when the Big Bug wasn't around and the herd was grazing.
He even remembered Lonna Lindquist showing him her perky boobs the week before he left for the Corps.

Oh, that white skin and those pink nip—

THUNK.

Bob hit the landing pad dead center. His rubber pistol landed in the horse trough.

The setup—cardboard boxes two high, topped with mattresses, topped again with an old pirate sail from some forgotten movie—did its job. Saved Bob from having Lonna's chest be his last earthly memory.

Of course, the trade-off was every molecule of air being knocked from his lungs. He saw double for a moment. Then he did what he always did after a bull threw him at the weekend rodeo:

Blow out the candle.
A slow breath in through the nose.
A focused exhale through pursed lips.

Worked like a charm.

He stood up, dusted off his pants, and accepted a lazy round of applause from the crew. The first hand he shook belonged to Hardtack—somehow already off the roof. Bob never could figure how he got down so fast.

The second unit director gave them a nod. The crew started breaking down, moving on to the next setup.

Bob turned in his duds to Wardrobe, headed to the Cashier with his voucher, then hopped on his surplus Harley with a check for $35 ($10 for the day, $25 for the fall gag), and the rest of his studio box lunch.

It was June 1955, and "Oklahoma" Bob Quigley was a rich young man.

He rode over the mountain into the San Fernando Valley, taking a dusty back road called Devonshire past the horse ranches, orange groves, and olive trees.
Then south on Sepulveda to a brand-new housing development called Panorama City.
He wondered how this place would look in fifty years.
He'd find out.

Bob lived off Sepulveda and Saticoy, in a square "Wingbat" style apartment with a blue pool in the middle. On weekends, pretty actresses would coat themselves in tan, poolside.

He didn't mind his roommate, David Silverstein, even when Davey peeked out the curtains at the weekend circus of fillies.

"Come on down with me, Davey, they won't bite."
"No, I don't have time today. Next time."

That time would never come.

David was a piano tuner—claimed he had perfect pitch, whatever that was.

One day, Bob found Davey's stash of *serious* porno mags. Illegal stuff, at least back then.
So it wasn't a surprise when, decades later, Bob ran into him and found out he'd made a mint owning a dozen adult bookstores in Hollywood and Downtown LA.

But that night, Bob was full of piss and vinegar. After a little pool time and a shower, he rode to the Palomino to meet up with Hardtack and the other stuntmen.

The Palomino wasn't just one of the many country bars around LA.
It was the crown jewel.

When Bob arrived, the lot was packed all the way down Lankershim.
The music was hot. The women were hotter.

Oklahoma Bob held his own.
Shots went up, shots went down.
He danced with any gal who'd have him, hollering like a wild man when each song ended.

He met a redhead named Wilkie and carried her over the hill to her shared apartment in Hollywood.
Same wingbat style. Same blue pool.
Same pretty actresses laying out.

He felt at home.

They fucked the rest of the night.

In the morning, Wilkie helped him pull on his boots and sent him off with a biscuit stuffed with syrup.

He'd never see her again, but he'd talk about Wilkie till his last breath.

Bob's first day as a Hollywood stuntman was done.

E. Peabody

He stared at himself in the mirror across the hooker's room, teetering on the edge of disgust at the man looking back.
What happened?
The cruel truth: nothing happened. He's always been disgusting.

He'd just forgotten how bad it was—how much nothing had changed—thanks to the tiny mirror above his bathroom sink back home. It's only good for shaving and digging the occasional plaster splinter out of his eye. His mirror didn't show him the truth—only gave him a way to get the specks out.

The plaster? That's courtesy of his upstairs neighbor, Jimbo—a sad drunk who comes alive every Saturday night, stomping through Motown hits like a washed-up go-go dancer. Every week, the ceiling sheds a fresh batch of dust and flakes, and somehow, without fail, the shit always finds its way into Peabody's eyes.

E. Peabody was a 50ish man who worked third shift at a city garbage site, manning the security gate. He kept to himself—a shut-in, if you will—and one day he confided in me that he hadn't touched another human in sixteen years.

On his 50th birthday, he got a broken-down prostitute to have sex with, just to have someone touch him.
He said he didn't even care about the sex. Said it was "like putting jumper cables on a dead battery."

One day soon after, Peabody just stopped. Stopped everything.
Stopped nodding to me in the hallway.
Stopped sitting in the lobby, waiting to go to work on his bicycle.
Stopped going to work.
And finally, stopped paying his $183-a-month rent.

Can a broken-down hooker stop a man dead in his tracks?
Not the ones on 94th and Fig.

The last Saturday night I saw Peabody was when he knocked on my door.
Nobody likes unannounced knocks on Skid Row.

I checked the peephole—E. Peabody.
He seemed surprised when I opened the door all the way. Something
he'd never do.

"What's up, dude?"
"Hey, six oh eight, thanks for opening your door."

Peabody had more than the usual plaster specks on his forehead and
shoulders.

"Fuck man, is Jimbo stomping around again?"
"God damn disco."
"Damn."

Peabody took a long pause, holding a full trash bag. He'd lost weight.
His clothes clung to him like orphans clinging to a sailor's leg.

"You know, six oh eight," he said. "I rather liked being invisible."

Then he turned and walked down the hallway to the garbage shaft.

That Tuesday, E. Peabody used his tiny mirror to cut his throat as the
eviction deputies kicked open his door.

Porn Stars as Heroes

"If any of you queerbaits call me Tony Bologna or Tony Pony, I'm gonna hop this counter and do a little Bronx two-step on your face. Comprende, motherfuckers?" Tony roared, slamming his baseball bat onto the front desk.

The threat was met with a chorus of wheezing laughter from the elderly lobby crew—old men laughing up what little air their lungs could muster. It sounded like a busted muffler shop.

Tony was in full performance mode. Finally, he had an audience—aged and wheezing, sure, but an audience nonetheless. He worked second shift at the hotel, from 2 p.m. to 10 p.m., the busiest and his favorite. The desk was his stage, and he played the role of foul-mouthed legend to perfection.

"It was '80 or '81," he'd begin. "I was 26, fresh outta the Navy— 'cause every porn story starts with 'I just got outta the Navy.' I'm back in the Bronx and bump into an old buddy I used to turn tricks with on 53rd."

"Wait—you were gay? Does Jennifer know this?"

"I ain't no fag, you queerbait," he snapped, chucking a balled-up Post-it note at my chest.

"Easy, baby. That one had juice," I said, ducking.

"How you even know about 53rd? You a chicken hawk?"

"I'm a Ramones fan. What can I say?"

Tony looked confused. "Ramones? What the fuck they gotta do with anything? Anyway, fuck it, I'll continue."

I held up my hands in mock surrender, enjoying the show.

"So, Rodney tells me there's a guy at the peep booth joint next to the Capri Theater on the Deuce looking for man talent. I head over, and this freaky dude's like, 'Hey man, can you get your dick hard right now?' Right there, in the lobby, people watching. I think about Lulu from Subic Bay, drop my pants, start cranking, and boom—hard as a rock. He goes, 'Finally! A real he-man. You're hired.'"

"That's one way to get a job." I offered.

Tony ignores me.

"And then I tell him I'm from Con-Ed, there to check his meter. Motherfucker nearly has a heart attack."

The muffler shop roared again. Even I cracked up. It was a great story—always was.

Tony Russo left the Bronx a month later after shooting a dozen or so loops—six-minute 8mm porn shorts that ran endlessly in peep booths. He was tired of getting stiffed—fifty bucks per loop, if he got paid at all. Word was San Francisco paid better.

He checked into a flop on the Tenderloin and started answering ads in local adult mags, using the patented "Lulu Technique" to prove his worth. Video hadn't taken over yet. Most productions were still on 16mm film, but the west coast producers paid more—especially the gay ones. The women made a few hundred a scene; the men, half that. Gay shoots paid triple.

"I didn't like it," he'd say, "but they treated me better. And the money? Forget it."

Tony always looked young—he credited Yiddish/Wop genetics. Age would catch up eventually, especially once crack entered the picture. But in the early days, he thrived. He earned a rep as a "Woodman"—a male performer who could get it up anytime, anywhere—and migrated south to the San Fernando Valley as it became porn's new capital.

And that's where the end began.

The parties were non-stop. Hollywood Hills, 24/7. Tony's charm and energy made him a popular invite.

"Big stars loved having a chump like me around. By the end of the night, they'd want me to fuck some girl while their friends snorted coke and cheered us on. I was a sideshow act. What the hell."

Even the gay parties had perks. Better coke. Flashier hosts. But they got darker. Young boys, sometimes clearly confused or misled, made appearances. Tony hated that part.

"I'd psych myself up. Do the scene. Cash the check. What the hell."

He dated a few women over the years—mostly girls from the biz. Civilian women didn't last long once they found out what he did for a living. One even threatened to sue him. The girls in the industry were their own breed—he'd joke that most would blow you for handing them a TV Guide. But the smart ones? The ones who had their shit together? He called them "the most dangerous animals in the kingdom."

Then came Penny.

She was from Ohio, mostly did girl-girl scenes—or so she told him. And for once, Tony fell hard. She was sweet, grounded, and didn't want anything from him. He even bought her a little Ohio Buckeye bracelet for Christmas.

They were together for just a few months. On his birthday, he got a call from her friend Diane, another actress. Penny had collapsed at the gym. Deep vein thrombosis.

He had to identify the body.

"She looked so small," he told me one night, quieter than usual. "Wasn't even sure it was her 'til I saw the bracelet. I still wear it. Right here."

He held up his wrist, and there it was.

By 1985, he was doing 10–15 scenes a month. By 1990, maybe three. The lifestyle caught up. AIDS loomed large. Work dried up.

He tried legit acting. Lasted nine seconds.

"In Hollywood, I was a freak show, not the main show."

So, like many retired porn actors, he drove a cab. That lasted three years. Then boredom kicked in. One night, he picked up a fare in a known drug zone and got caught smoking crack with the guy.

Arrested. Fired. Skid Row.

The Holy Trinity.

Tony bounced around SROs, taking whatever jobs, he could find. Eventually, he got clean. Got a job working hotel security, then the desk. The owners liked him—protective nature, charm with the elderly residents. He thought about doing stand-up, but why bother? The lobby muffler shop was a built-in audience.

Around 2005, he started making runs to Tijuana. Steroid smuggling. A new hustle. He had dreams—buying a house, maybe even retiring with a little dignity.

And then he vanished, never coming back across the Border.

One day he was there, protecting the coffee machine. The next, gone.

No goodbye.

No trace.

Just a story waiting to be retold in the lobby, one more time.

Baglady (circa Crabby Joe's)

I look closer at the woman—
closer than she'd like me to
have looked.

I tried to see
her soul leave—
the way the Indians said it happens,
to brag how backward those whites are,
they never see the soul
leave.

I walked closer,
stepping over the glass.
On the glass—
her body,
the last breath.

Women don't like close inspection
when they're not ready—
no makeup,
unusual position.
Compromising.

Her soul refused to leave,
wasn't ready.
I was that close.
I could only stand,

hands in pockets,
watching—
staring past her eyes.

I couldn't tell how pretty she was,
if she was.
It was important
to her, I'm sure.

But death was taking her,
awkward or not,
makeup or none.
She was dying.

I looked closer,
to see her eyes—
maybe that's where the soul
exits.

Crouched closer,
closer.
Perfectly still,
looking—
not wanting her to move,
knowing death
had come and gone
that quick.

No matter how
close I looked,
how soon I arrived,
she was gone.

She was gone before the car had hit her—
cartwheeling,
tumbling—

one shoe
resting on a truck.

I looked back at the space
between
her shell and the impact.

Perhaps her soul was still
there,
not yet caught up—
still lagging,
caught off guard.

Or just relieved
it's finally over.

Oklahoma Bob Pt. 2
(When the World Turned Different)

"Oklahoma" Bob Quigley could never quite remember what first drew him to Genora Esposito. Was it her full-lipped, dazzling smile? Or the way her tight sweaters hugged that busty figure she was proud to flaunt? Either way, Bob always claimed it was John Wayne who introduced them.

It was August 1959. Bob was scraping by as a Hollywood stuntman, mostly off rather than on. That month, however, John Wayne had set off for Texas to film his epic *The Alamo*, and in doing so, vacuumed up most of the working cowboy stuntmen in town. Bob remembered the long convoy: trucks, campers, sedans pulling horse trailers, all rolling down Route 66 like a low-budget cavalry.

But Bob didn't go to Texas. He stayed loyal to his buddy Hartack Delmonte, a lead stunt gaffer still cranking out Westerns for the scrappier independent studios. With the major talent pool drained, Bob found himself in high demand. For three golden months, he and Hartack feasted—three, sometimes four stunt jobs a day. He wore out his Chevy racing between Burbank, Universal, and the West Valley ranches.

One day, coming back from Spawn Ranch, he stopped at a Woolworth's in the north valley for a cheeseburger. He was halfway through it when a voice behind him said, "Excuse me, mister, are you a cowboy?"

He turned to see a brunette bombshell—tight red sweater, knockout smile, five-foot-two and pure dynamite.

Her name was Genora. She was a cashier, 18, fresh from Cleveland. When asked why she'd moved to L.A. with no job, no friends, and no plan, she'd shrug and say, "It was something different."

They married four months later and honeymooned in Hawaii, staying at Jimmy Stewart's ranch. She fell hard for the charming cowboy.

By the next year, Genora—now known affectionately as GQ—was assistant floor manager at Woolworth's and taking business classes at community college. They bought a ranch-style home near Victory Blvd. Cookouts and cocktail parties became the norm. Sometimes Bob snagged invites to movie premieres and brought GQ, who would talk about it for days afterward.

Then, in 1966, everything changed.

Bob was coming home late from a shoot when a drunk driver ran a red light and hit his Harley. Bob was thrown under a parked truck. The driver fled. Cops inspected the abandoned bike, not realizing Bob lay broken just feet away. He was found 30 minutes later.

He woke up in the hospital. GQ was at his bedside.

The injuries were catastrophic: a shattered left leg, busted hip, fractured arm, and spinal trauma.

Bob would later say, "Sometimes the end comes for you, and you don't know it for years."

After seven months of painful recovery, stunt work was out of the question. He took a job as a maintenance man for RCA in Northridge. He quietly developed a dependence on Percodan, but GQ had already drifted.

She was young, ambitious, tired of playing nursemaid to a man who now shuffled instead of swaggered. She stayed late at work. She went out drinking. When Bob confronted her, her fiery Italian temper would explode. She accused *him* of cheating. Plates flew.

One night, he followed her to a tiki bar. She met a slick-looking guy with a Porsche. When they embraced outside, Bob calmly raised a pistol and fired. The bullet missed her head by an inch.

He served four years in San Quentin. She divorced him.

When he got out, his old friend Jimmy Stewart—now a full-bird colonel in the Air Force—called in a favor and got Bob his job back at RCA. He traded Percodan for prison pruno, then upgraded to good vodka.

In 1970, he moved into an apartment in Van Nuys. Lived alone. Retired on his union pension.

He almost remarried in 1985—a lovely Filipina he met at the horse track. But when asked why they didn't tie the knot, Bob would shrug: "We met at a horse track."

They lived together until spring 1991, when she stabbed him in the chest and fled to Mexico. Thought he was cheating. He wasn't. He swore.

With his eyesight failing and no interest in assisted living, Bob moved to downtown L.A. He landed at the Baltimore Hotel—cheap rent, private bath, and the King Eddy bar just across the street.

There, Bob became part of the furniture. A fixture in the bar and lobby, telling stories to anyone who'd listen.

He died in the mid-2000s of Huntington's disease, which he'd quietly battled for 15 years. Only his doctor and his favorite paramedics knew.

His stories often returned to Spawn Movie Ranch—later infamous for its ties to the Manson Family. Bob had shot countless Westerns there, including his first gig with Hartack in 1955. He would talk about the bars and clubs running late into the night and the house parties in the Hills. He talked about a red head named Wilkie and asked about her on his death bed. He said those early days were the last time he felt the world made sense.

After Bob's cremation, his friend Mark—a fellow resident of the Baltimore—took the urn to Spawn Ranch one night. He buried it deep in the dirt, one eye looking out for rattlesnakes, and toasted Oklahoma Bob with a swig of fine vodka.

The cowboy rode off, one last time, into the dust.

My Life as a Gutter

Finally, the rain
Even Skid Row baths
Water cleanses, no one
Is missed.

You see the needed
Purification, you
Feel the unwanted
Of it.

Sometimes impure
Must stay impure
To keep its purity
The Tiger murders
To stay a tiger.

Skid Row will let
The rain wash and
Scrub the streets
Once, twice, three

Times per annum
It never is clean
To live, just to
Breathe and pump
Blood for its host.

You stand and watch
Needles, condoms,
Baggies swept away
It's owners already

Stocked. Don't lean
Into the gutter to
See life draining
You'll fall in
You'll see.

West Is Always Better Than East of Where You Are (in L.A.)

Mark lives on Skid Row.

It really isn't all that bad.

One night, Mark saw a black bum lay right down in the gutter—right there on 5th and Los Angeles.

If you know anything about Skid Row, you know that's one nasty kick of concrete.

Bastard piss, orphaned sperm, and other forgotten refuse line the angled cement, all fused into a smell distinct to this one brutal square of the city.

Mark watched as the man squatted, placed a hand down, then slowly lowered the rest of his body into that obscene manger.

He let out a long breath, then went completely still.

Later, Mark would swear the man's body *absorbed* the concrete—or maybe it absorbed him.

Mark doesn't cringe much. But this shook his soul hard enough that he briefly thought about going back to his old lady.

He walked over.

"Hey man, don't lay in that shit," he said. "That's fucking nasty."

He started to extend his hand.

"Papa Doe don't need no help, you white devil."

The guy barely moved his lips, but it came out so clear that Mark looked around to see if someone else had said it.

"What?" (Mark's comebacks are legendary.)

"Fuck you, honky. Devil-mutha' fucka."

"Hey, man—it's cool. I just don't think anybody, even a nigga, should be laying down in this shit."

"NIGGA"!" the man yelled, eyes snapping open. "You mutha—"

Before he could finish or unstick himself, Mark short-kicked him in the temple.

His head bounced off the concrete. His eyes fluttered. He melted deeper into his little hive, just as some serious Crip motherfuckers rounded the corner.

Oh shit.

"...and Aaliyah wasn't no whore!" Mark shouted at the unconscious man. "She had more talent than any white bitch out there, you race traitor!"

The Crips walked on, nodding their approval.

The Skid Row Library

In the yellowed nook of Skid Row's den,
A battered shelf, unsteady, worn—
It leans beneath forgotten men,
Their silent stories, whiskey-sworn.

Old white faces, hollow-eyed,
Pore through pages, truths denied—
Of bottle dreams and tinfoil schemes,
Of vanished gods and outlawed beams.

Books stacked high with crooked grace:
Jack London's ice, Homer's face,
Raymond Carver's glassy ache,
Hammett's shadows, hard to shake.
Fact and fiction intertwine,
Sci-fi pulses, fringe align.

Where secrets mumble, barely heard—
Bigfoot's print, the raven's word,
Tales from prison's iron breath,
Cold-case ghosts and wrongful death,
Loch Ness stirs the midnight air,
Area 51 blinks somewhere.

The shelf groans low, half-collapsed with sin,
Steeped in smoke and spilled-out gin.
The musk of pulp, of lust and lore,

Of dime-store love and lost rapport.
Soft-core whispers, grease-stained sleeves,
Truth and myth between the leaves.

Here, in literature's rough embrace,
Greatness squats in a broken place.
Take, then leave — no questions asked,
A temple masked in whiskey's flask.
For souls adrift, both cracked and kind,
This shelf still guards the poet's mind.

Porn Stars as Heroes (Pt. 2)

You Can't Sleep

Your eyes pop open just before 3 a.m. Was it the scream down the hall, or the one from outside? Or maybe it was your mind again, reminding you how close you are to the sidewalk—really being homeless.

Now you know the truth about the wild things. They're your neighbors now.

The bed isn't yours. It's been used by untold dozens, doing God knows what. Sleeping, drinking, smoking, shooting up, pissing, shitting, and cumming. They just change the sheets—ish.

Now here you are, in this single room. A single room with four doors across three walls.

On one wall is the main door. It creaks when people walk by, and you have zero confidence in its locking abilities. Your bed sits against a second door—painted shut long before you were born. On the third wall is your closet door, and by closet you mean a space barely big enough for a stack of phone books. Next to that is another door, also locked and painted shut. You've pushed a low chest of drawers in front of it, its mirror not original to the model.

When you open the drawers, you catch the scent of seventy years of forgotten stories. Pants, socks, shirts—some neatly folded, some tossed in with no concern for how they'll represent their owner. Sometimes you wonder if they hid their guns, drugs, or cash under the underwear, like you do.

The fourth wall is where the windows live. Right now, they face an interior airshaft, so when you look out, all you see are your opposite numbers—sometimes, a version of yourself twenty years from now, staring right back. You smile. Gotta be neighborly.

You have to tilt your head up to glimpse a patch of sky. It reminds you of jail, so you don't do it often.

The concrete floor is painted red. The paint chips and sticks to your bare feet, revealing the gray underneath—another reminder of how close you are to becoming a wild thing.

You look up a lot. The ceiling's been plastered so many times it's formed a three-dimensional map of the Saharan Desert. Hey, look—there's Lawrence of Arabia.

A lone fire sprinkler keeps sentinel in the center, extending down from a boarded-up transom above your door. You'd kill to have that transom back. It might cool off your room, even if it meant getting burned alive while you slept off a good drunk. It seems worth it.

So, you sit up in your used bed, place your feet on the chipping floor, and stand.

Shadows pass the bottom of your door—people heading to the bathroom. Your bathroom too.

You throw on some clothes, lock your door, check it twice, and head downstairs to the lobby.

The building's an old hotel from 1910, built for the middle class. It was advertised as fireproof. It's been through countless changes, but still holds to its purpose.

The lobby is vast. The desk clerk can see every inch of it—and the trouble coming from the outside. The check-in counter sits at the far end. A once-ornate staircase passes to the left, the elevator to the right. A decent clerk will stop non-residents from coming upstairs and cutting your throat.

Usually.

You descend the stairs and grab one of the two dozen somewhat comfortable chairs; all angled toward the glass wall facing Los Angeles Street.

Soon you see why. It's a nonstop parade of humanity—going east and west to score, or north and south to scout. Everyone is high, lit, strung out, or tweaking. Drunk, sometimes, but that's so 1980s. The old bums are dying out.

You're surrounded by the last of a dying breed—white, drunk, single older males. Some have been here for thirty years. Most are just spending their final ones watching what was or could be them outside that glass.

Behind you is the entrance to the pubic-hair-infested basement laundromat. On the wall next to that—opposite the desk clerk—is the Hotel Library. An old four-tier wooden shelf, five feet wide, stacked with books and magazines. A handmade sign reads: "Read one, leave one." Seems fair.

You browse the selection and are amazed by the depth. Hemingway, Céline, Burroughs, Plath, Spillane, Carver, Hammett, Chandler, Christie (lots), Fitzgerald, Faulkner, Steinbeck, Orwell, Vonnegut, Crichton, King, McCarthy, Grisham. Even the old gods: Kafka, Chekhov, Tolstoy, Tolkien, Boccaccio—and your favorite, Hamsun.

Once in a while, you'll see Bukowski, Fante, or Willy Shakespeare, but they get snatched up quick, never to return. Same with the porn mags.

Then there are the piles of old *Time, Life, People, Rolling Stone, Popular Mechanics*, and every conspiracy mag known to man. If it reeks of cigarettes, it came from Carlos Huerta's private stash.

The bottom shelf is a canyon of pulpy gold.

You once left a copy of *Pynchon*. It sat untouched for seven years.

A vending machine and a coffee machine sit next to the elevator. Both are well-stocked, well-maintained, and priced fairly. Sometimes, they're lifesavers.

One night, a non-resident kicked the coffee machine. He was swarmed by cane-wielding geriatrics who knew no mercy. One even shoved a gun in his mouth. The desk clerk, Tony—an ex-porn star—had to break it up while laughing his ass off, saving the man's life.

So, you grab a coffee, take a seat, snatch a UFO magazine that smells like ancient nicotine, and think about your door lock.

Then you watch the wild things go by.

Encore une fois, très loin en bas

In the hesitant fall of rain,
Skid Row weeps in silence—
its scars mapped by water,
its cleansing just a rumor.

The streets are rinsed,
but the ghosts remain—
stains that remember,
a purity born of pain.

A tiger stirs in the alley,
its growl raw and real—
a feral need to survive,
even if it devours itself.

They wash the sidewalks
once, twice, again—
but the grime holds on,
like breath on the edge.

Needles whisper promises,
baggies drift like lost prayers—
fragments of someone's yesterday
slipping through the cracks.

Don't peer too close to the gutter—
the drain remembers faces.
Fall in,
and you might not come back.

Plagues I Have
Known While Yachting

I've never been known for my timing.

At eleven, I walked in on my parents going at it doggie style to Stevie Wonder. *Superstition* has never sounded the same since.

In middle school, I interrupted our baseball team's pitcher and catcher switching positions in the shower. Turns out "Don't drop the soap" jokes were never that funny.

And in 2001, on the way to a job interview, I stopped for a quick chat with Dave Crazy and Big Sammy out front of the Baltimore. We watched an armored car roll by and turn down a side street. Minutes later, police were swarming. The truck had hit a pothole and dropped a bag of cash. It was right on my route to the interview.

I missed out on a $200,000 payday. Some do-gooder found the bag and turned it in two days later out of guilt. The bank gave him five grand. After taxes.

I'm finally moving out of the Baltimore after nineteen years. Why did I stay that long? I'm just as mystified as you. I can only offer something weak like, "Time flies," or, "Life just gets in the way."

Of course, my timing couldn't be better. I sign a new one-year lease with a 271.51% rent increase—and the whole planet shuts down for Plague Lite: COVID.

I'd actually committed to leaving back in 2008. Then I caught a case of swine flu. Passed out and woke up with blue lips. Put things in perspective. Life on the Westside could wait. If I survived—which the doctors said was 40/60.

Two years later, I made another commitment—but then came the bedbugs. A full-on invasion. And the recession was still raging. Work dried up. Money vanished.

So, I stayed. I fought the good fight against *Cimex lectularius* and gave up more than I bargained for. One thing I know for sure: after bedbugs, swine flu doesn't seem so bad.

By then, all the OGs I'd known were gone. Dead, relocated, or vanished into myth. I still wonder who got off easy.

Fall 2016, I get taken for thousands in a car sale scam. Should've seen it coming, but I wanted to get my daughter a cool ride. Got the money back just in time—but the Father of the Year trophy melted right along with my hubris.

Then came 2020. My year to move. I came to that decision after suffering a heart attack on January 3rd. The kind they call "The Widowmaker."

What was I thinking? Ringing in the new year like a young sailor on leave in Shanghai.

Would I do it again?

Yeah. It was a hell of a night.

So, I made a serious commitment to the housing gods of L.A. And they responded with a sweet 800-square-foot one-bedroom near Culver City. Gated parking and everything. My faith had paid off.

But I forgot—gods love their little jokes.

Just like everybody else, I rode out the plague, always thinking, "I'll go back to work next month. Once the curve flattens."

We all know how *that* turned out.

In 2022, I returned to a job I had no business returning to. Too much weight. Bad knees. And the gig now meant late nights with L.A.'s *young nouveau riche*. It chewed me up.

Now it's 2025. The King Eddy is long gone. The Baltimore's been turned into a charity housing HIV patients. I look back on all the people I met in those nineteen years on Skid Row, and I always think of Joe.

Joe was an average guy who made some bad decisions. Lived wild. Slept rough near the Baltimore. I'd see him every day. Gave him a couple bucks when I could. He was never pushy. Always polite.

One day I asked him, "What's the worst part of being homeless?"

He said, "The first two weeks. They're terrifying. You don't sleep. You try to stay off the concrete, away from the rats. But then you figure it out—the unwritten rules. How to keep one step ahead of trouble. Takes about two weeks. And if you make it… it starts to feel almost normal. So normal, you can't even remember when it changed. It just becomes home."

And that's what I think back to.

Not as bad as Joe had it—but I remember those first few weeks. Fighting that hotel, fighting the people, staying up all night while others laughed and lived. Then at some point… I stopped fighting.

Somewhere along the way, I learned the unwritten rules.

Couldn't tell you exactly when—but one day, it just felt like home.

My home.

Acknowledgments

To my daughter, Erika—thank you for giving me that purpose. You're the reason I kept going, and the reason I keep going still.

To my closest friend, Sarah Higginbotham—thank you for always being on my side, especially when I was wrong. That's when it matters most.

To Susanna Isidoro—our weekly dates kept my creative spark lit, even when the rest of the world went dim. Thank you.

To my writer's group, *The Agents of [sic]*—thanks for the encouragement, the feedback, and for drinking all of my bourbon. Every drop was worth it.

To Geo Beltran, Rich and Carlos Rivera—for always having my back, no matter what.

To Mongo, for keeping an old dog in the kitchen. *Vive le sacre mercenaire!*

And to Anny Grandson—for never giving up on her journey which is what inspired me.

I couldn't have done this without you freaks.

Michael W. Corcoran

Coming soon:

LIVE NUDE, NUDES

Stories of LA's Strip Clubs

By

Michael W.Corcoran

Author's Page

The author is a long-standing advocate of the human race, although his experience with Hollywood leaves him questioning that.

He hails from Raleigh, N.C. by way of Findlay, Ohio, and has been a dedicated Angeleno since 1997.

His turn-ons: Long drives to nowhere with good music, old biker movies, and drinking in bars.

His turn-offs: Hairy backs and rude people.

Michael has worked in all kinds of bars over the past 40+ years, in many different roles—usually ending his shift with the words, *"Ma'am, please put down the dwarf."*

He loves to read, especially Dashiell Hammett, Knut Hamsun, Steve Martin (the banjo player), and poetry by Dan Fante.

His musical tastes run the gamut, but lately he's been sticking to safe choices like HurtHawks, Johnny Paycheck, and Mozart.

He lives for jiu-jitsu, and he too wonders why he still sucks.

At the time of this writing, the author is on sabbatical (read: unemployed).

www.ingramcontent.com/pod-product-compliance
Lightning Source LLC
Chambersburg PA
CBHW060331310726
48976CB00007B/2523